"I should j[ust]... summer?"

"Why not?" Josias asked. "You work for me for three months and you'll have money to take with you. And if your family thinks we're engaged, that'll give them time to get used to the idea that you even draw. Because...they don't know, do they?"

There was no hiding the truth in those big turquoise eyes. Naomi's family had no idea she wanted to go to art school.

"This way they can become accustomed to the idea that you have this hobby at all. And then eventually that you want to turn it into something different, perhaps more. Give them the summer, work for me, save your money, and in the fall..." He allowed his voice to trail off.

"In the fall I go to school."

"Jah," he said the word, but it was choked.

She heaved a great sigh. "Just for the summer, right?" she asked.

Josias's heart kicked up a notch. "*Jah*, just for the summer."

She stuck her hand out to shake his. "Well then, Josias Schrock, you've got yourself a deal."

Born and bred in Mississippi, **Amy Lillard** is a transplanted Southern belle who now lives in Oklahoma with her deputy husband and two spoiled cats. When she's not creating happy endings, she's an avid football fan (go Chiefs!) and an adoring mother to an almost-adult son and loves binge-watching television shows. Amy is an award-winning author with more than sixty novels and novellas in print. She loves to hear from readers. You can find her on Facebook, Instagram, X, Goodreads, TikTok and Pinterest. You can email her at amylillard@hotmail.com or check out her website, amywritesromance.com.

Books by Amy Lillard

Love Inspired

The Amish Christmas Promise
The Amish Bachelor's Promise
The Amish Nanny's Secret

Visit the Author Profile page at LoveInspired.com.

THE AMISH NANNY'S SECRET

AMY LILLARD

If you purchased this book without a cover you should be aware that this book is stolen property. It was reported as "unsold and destroyed" to the publisher, and neither the author nor the publisher has received any payment for this "stripped book."

ISBN-13: 978-1-335-62114-6

The Amish Nanny's Secret

Copyright © 2025 by Amy Lillard

All rights reserved. No part of this book may be used or reproduced in any manner whatsoever without written permission.

Without limiting the author's and publisher's exclusive rights, any unauthorized use of this publication to train generative artificial intelligence (AI) technologies is expressly prohibited.

This is a work of fiction. Names, characters, places and incidents are either the product of the author's imagination or are used fictitiously. Any resemblance to actual persons, living or dead, businesses, companies, events or locales is entirely coincidental.

For questions and comments about the quality of this book, please contact us at CustomerService@Harlequin.com.

® is a trademark of Harlequin Enterprises ULC.

Love Inspired
22 Adelaide St. West, 41st Floor
Toronto, Ontario M5H 4E3, Canada
www.LoveInspired.com

Printed in Lithuania

Commit thy way unto the Lord; trust also in him;
and he shall bring it to pass.
—*Psalms* 37:5

To all the dreamers, may you find your true way,
whatever it may be.

Chapter One

Why weren't the wedding guests going home? It had been hours. Hours past time for the event to be over, and everyone was still milling around, still drinking lemonade and iced tea, still eating the chicken and filling and wedding cake and pie—what there was left of it—and just…hanging out. Still.

Naomi Ebersol checked the clock her *dat* had hung outside on the back porch to help them keep track of the time when they were out in the yard. Right now, it was simply showing Naomi that the wedding should have ended a long time ago. She smoothed her hand down her periwinkle blue dress and white apron made especially for her sister's wedding.

As their tradition, Mattie and Samuel's wedding was held at her family's home. Not the home Mattie had shared with David, her first husband, but the one she had grown up in. It was a lovely property with a large yard complete with budding fruit trees and pecking hens, all adding to the beauty and serenity of the wedding.

Thomas Ebersol, their father, had moved into the home a year after marrying Anna Grace Weaver, his beautiful blond-haired fiancée. Together they had raised six daughters until Anna Grace's untimely death when Naomi was only thirteen. It was a terrible age to lose a parent, especially a mother, and Naomi had turned to the only thing that could offer her solace: a sketch pad. A *verboten* sketch pad.

That had been twelve years ago, and right now, Naomi had to figure out what to do about the fifty or so straggling wedding guests who had somehow forgotten that second weddings were supposed to be shorter than first ones. There was no second meal, and the event only lasted half a day instead of on into the evening hours. Everyone knew that, even today's overzealous revelers.

Naomi supposed that their tiny Amish community was just happy to see Mattie and Samuel tie the knot. Mattie had been through so much, losing her husband David while pregnant and somehow taking care of her other two girls and her goat farm through it all. Samuel had come back into the fold after many years away. He had rejoined the church and was welcomed back with open arms. *Jah*, it was some coincidence that Samuel was also David's twin. But everyone was glad to see them happy and settled. So glad that no one batted an eye when they moved their nuptials up to have a rare May wedding.

Maybe that was why people were lingering. *Jah*, they were happy for the blessed couple, but the weather was also spectacular. The sun was shining, and the sky was blue, and everything seemed absolutely perfect.

Except—

They were running out of food, and frankly Naomi was tired. And she was worried that her sister and Samuel would have no time alone to celebrate their union if someone didn't do something…and quick. Someone like her.

She marched over to where her twin, Priscilla, was holding one of her own twin daughters. Leona and Lallie looked so much alike that without a direct line to her face, Naomi couldn't tell which one her sister held. Whichever twin this was, Naomi was sure that their younger sister Lizzie had the other one.

"What are we going to do?" Naomi asked Priscilla.

Priscilla eyed her balefully and shifted the small toddler into a more comfortable position in her arms. After the adjustment, Naomi could see that she held Lallie. "About what?"

"So many people are still here. Don't you think they need to go home? Shouldn't we *do* something?" Naomi resisted the urge to tap her foot as she waited for her sister to answer.

As far as twins went, she and Priscilla were about as different as two women could be and still claim to be kin. It was as if the pair of them did everything in their power to annoy and contradict the other. If Naomi wore a blue dress, Priscilla wore pink. If Naomi wanted to play cards, Priscilla wanted to go for a walk. Naomi even wondered if that was why Priscilla had accepted Mark Raber's proposal when she was barely twenty. They married two years later, and he died two years after that, leaving Priscilla to raise their babies on her own.

"No. I don't think we should do anything."

"You don't think—" Naomi couldn't believe her ears. "It's been hours," she calmly explained. Getting upset wouldn't solve anything. She just needed to know what to do. "We're running out of food, and almost everyone is still here."

Priscilla shifted the baby once more, and Naomi knew that the little girl, though still so young, had to be getting heavy.

"People are having a good time. Unless Mattie and Samuel complain, what point is there? It's their wedding."

She hated when her sister got all pragmatic.

"Maybe everyone's not finished talking about Freeman and Evie," Priscilla added.

Priscilla was right about that one, whether Naomi wanted to admit it or not. The wedding gave their district a firsthand look at the new couple to go along with all the gossip floating around Millers Creek about Freeman Yoder and their sister Evie.

It all started when Helen Schrock had broken her engagement with Freeman to go off and live with the fancy Amish of Lancaster County. Freeman was best friends with Evie, and somehow a romance had started. Then Helen returned. For a moment everyone held their breath wondering if Freeman would throw over Evie and go back to Helen, but as far as Naomi knew, Freeman and Evie were still planning their December wedding. *Jah*, there was a lot to talk about these days. But not much food to have while talking about it.

"So, what do we do about feeding everyone?"

"How can we be running out of food? We made pans... *trays* of chicken and filling. And you're telling me that it's all gone?"

"Jah." Naomi almost wilted in relief. Finally, Priscilla understood the trouble they were in.

"That cannot be possible." Priscilla shook her head.

"I've seen the food table. I've checked in the house. It's gone, and no one appears to be leaving."

Lack of food aside, they needed to have time to clean up and get something to eat for themselves. Then Mattie's girls would stay there at their *dawdi*'s house while the newlyweds went back to Mattie's to enjoy a little bit of marital bliss. Well, after they milked the goats. Dairy farming didn't stop just because a person got married.

Their cousins Faith and Lillianna had gone over this morning to help with the milking, but once Mattie and Samuel got back home tonight, they were on their own.

"I mean, they are setting up the horseshoe pitch." *They* being several of the younger wedding guests, but there were enough of the older crowd around to supervise. Or prevent. Yet no one seemed concerned. "Do I need to go out there and tell all these…*people* that the wedding is over, and it's time for them to all leave?"

"Naomi?"

She whirled around at the sound of the unfamiliar voice.

No, that wasn't true. The voice was somewhat familiar, but it wasn't the voice she had been expecting to hear.

"Josias!" She pressed a hand to her heart. "You startled me." How much had he heard? And where was her sister? "I was just talking to Priscilla." Naomi's words were breathless and apologetic. She didn't understand how her sister could move that quickly. Or maybe the day was simply getting to her.

"I see." He didn't sound like he did. He sounded…a bit put out. And after what she had said… "Have you seen Esther? I'm guessing it's past time to go home."

Naomi briefly closed her eyes, but when she opened them again everything was just as it had been. The sky was still blue, the wedding guests were still pitching horseshoes, and Josias Schrock was still staring at her as if she were the rudest person he had ever met. "I didn't mean that," she said. And it was the truth. She had just been going off at the mouth and not watching what she was saying. Her *dat* was always telling her—and Mattie told her, too—that one day she was going to say the wrong thing to the wrong person and feelings were going to get hurt, friendships ruined, lives forever altered.

"It's all right. I'm sorry we've inconvenienced you. I just need to find Esther so I can take her home."

"Please." Naomi hated that she sounded so desperate, but if Mattie found out, she would be horrified that Naomi had made Josias leave. Mattie and Samuel were better friends with the man than she was. He was closer to their age, after all. He had married young and had almost a half dozen kids before his wife fell ill and died. Now here Naomi was kicking him out of the wedding.

Josias stopped at her words, tilted his head to one side and stared at her. "Are you all right?"

She closed her eyes once more, just briefly, as she nodded. If Priscilla was still standing close, her twin would have told her that she was worrying too much. She had been worrying a lot these days, over one thing or another. "*Jah*. I'm fine. This wedding has just been…" She allowed her words to trail off. Let him fill in the blank with whatever suited him best. Naomi's top picks were: *not as much fun as it looked, stressful beyond belief* and *more trouble than it was worth*.

Okay, so that last one was a little harsh. But even as large as their family was, the brunt of the wedding seemed to fall on her. Or maybe it just felt that way. Maybe, come tomorrow, after a full night's sleep, she would think differently about the whole thing.

"I'm pretty sure I saw Esther over on the front porch."

Talking with a gaggle of girls including Naomi's cousin Faith and sister Evie. No doubt they were planning out Evie's own wedding.

How Naomi wished she could be so carefree. Up until the last couple of months, she had felt that lighthearted spirit, but then it seemed as if things were changing, and they were leaving her behind. Mattie had found love again. Evie was set to marry Freeman. Priscilla had her twins. What did Naomi have?

Nothing but secret drawings and the expected job of helping her sisters. She didn't mind it, but there had to be more. Which was why she filled out the application to Moore College of Art & Design in Philadelphia. Not that she actually expected to be accepted. They were one of the top schools for art in the country. And she had never had any formal training. Of course not. Her community frowned on this sort of study. No one in her family knew she had such a talent. She had never shown anyone. Not even her sisters. Maybe that was why she was so jumpy lately.

She pushed the thought away. That was something she could think about later. When wedding guests weren't staying long past time for a second wedding to be over.

Josias nodded, though the action seemed a bit reluctant, as if he wasn't sure that he should leave her to her own devices. *"Danki."* He started to turn away.

"You're not leaving because of what I said, *jah*?"

"Of course not." He smiled and left to find his sister.

Naomi watched him go, biting her lip and hoping that it was only the stress getting to her. Otherwise, she was turning into a person that she didn't want to be.

Chapter Two

"Are you sure you're going to be okay?"

Josias turned toward his sister Esther and smiled reassuringly. At least he hoped the action was reassuring. His confidence had shifted a bit with everything that was going on. Yesterday it seemed as if he had a plan and God was helping him see it through, and today everything was falling apart...er, changing. "Dat needs you more. I understand."

And he did. He didn't like it, but he understood. He was an adult, and it was time to stand on his own feet. To quit relying on his sisters for every meal that crossed his table. But it had been hard, these months since Marie had died. Frankly, it had been difficult before she had died as well. He had put off finding a permanent solution in favor of licking his wounds and trying to heal what remained of his family. But now Helen and their mother were taking a trip to Western Pennsylvania, leaving Josias, his father, Elmer, and Josias's brother, Levi, to fend for themselves. Or rather with only Esther to make sure they ate and had clean clothes. And since Josias was the only one who didn't live in the same house, he was now having to figure out his own solution.

"Jah." Esther frowned. The recent events had been hard

on all of them. Not just Marie's death, but Helen's troubles as well.

As if breaking up with her long-time boyfriend, Freeman, wasn't enough to shake up the family, his older sister Helen had run away to Lancaster County to see how the fancier Amish lived only to return in the family way. He knew the phrase was old-fashioned to a fault, but he couldn't think of his sister, the same girl he had played with, swam with, did practically everything with when they were children, as preg—the *P* word. No, he couldn't even allow it in his thoughts. And when the rest of Millers Creek found out…the fallout would surely be swift and harsh.

But it was true. No matter how any of them felt about it.

Josias himself got all of the drama secondhand from Esther, who had taken over the care of his children while Helen had been away. Now Helen and their mother had gone to New Wilmington—Josias presumed so Helen could stay there with extended family until the baby was born. According to Esther, Helen had refused to reveal who the father of the baby was and declared that she was going to raise the child herself.

Of course, at first everyone thought that it had to be Freeman's child, but she vehemently denied it, and no matter how hard their father pressed, she would not tell her secret. Then with her stunning announcement that she would rather face excommunication and worse if she kept the baby after everything was said and done…well, his family had been rocked to the core.

His mother had whisked Helen away to the other side of the state, leaving Esther to care for their father and Josias to fend for himself. And his boys of course.

They were too young to understand any of what was going on, but Josias was worried that this current shake-up was going to send them all into a spiral. They might not understand, but they did know that their mother was gone, their aunt Helen was gone, and now their aunt Esther was abandoning them as well. At least he hoped they didn't feel abandoned. Yet how could they not? Every few weeks and months something happened to change their world practically beyond their comprehension.

He sighed and felt his sister's gaze land on him. He hadn't meant to sound so melancholy.

"I'll be fine, Esther. *We'll* be fine," he emphasized. Though the confidence in his voice was forced. They would have to be fine because they didn't have another choice. It was time he solved his own life problems.

Except the true answer was to get remarried. And that wasn't something he was ready for yet. He didn't know if he ever would be.

He swung down from the carriage and smiled once again at his sister, hoping to dispel her fears and concern over his family. Every one of the Schrocks had more to be concerned about than was easily handled, and he needed to remove all that he could from her shoulders.

"How was the wedding?" his *dat* asked as he came out of the house. He held the youngest of Josias's boys on his hip. At two years old, Tommy was showing his independence, kicking his legs in an attempt to get down and run to his father. The other boys filed out of the house behind their *dawdi*.

"Fine," Josias said, knowing the answer was vapid. "Happy." But he knew what was coming next, if not now, then soon. His own lecture on the benefits of getting remarried. It had barely been a year since Marie had died. He wasn't ready for such a step.

The love he saw between Mattie and Samuel was enviable. Even with the reserved nature of Amish couples, it still shone through. He couldn't say he'd had that sort of connection with Marie, and since her death…it made him feel guilty. Like he hadn't made the best of the time that he'd had with her.

"All right. All right." His father gave a weary sigh that might have even been part groan and set Tommy on his feet. Josias's youngest ran pell-mell toward him, red head down as he sped up and grabbed Josias around the legs.

Josias swung the boy into his arms and hugged him close. He wasn't going to continue making those mistakes that he had made with his wife. He was doing his very best to savor every moment and hold it close because those moments could be so fleeting. *Jah*, it was all part of God's will, but when His plan was enforced, Josias needed to be able to say that he had done all that he could. Unlike his relationship with Marie.

The rest of his boys came out to join him, the oldest two, Dale and Eli, chattering about what they had done while Josias had been gone. Dale was particularly animated, at least for him. The eldest of his boys tended to be more solemn these days, as if starting school was serious business. He supposed that for a six-year-old it was. At least that was when Josias thought the change had occurred. Though it probably had more to do with Marie's death in those weeks before.

As far as looks, his boys were mostly a mishmash of his

and Marie's coloring. Dale boasted the same dark hair as Josias and the pale blue eyes of his mother. Five-year-old Eli was blond like his mother but had Josias's own gray-blue eyes. Four-year-old Harley was the spitting image of Josias, while three-year-old Ivan took after his mother. Then there was Tommy, who was his own person for sure and for certain.

Josias did his best to listen to his boys' babble while waving goodbye to his father and sister. Once again he was all alone with his children. He missed having Helen or Esther or his mother around. He liked the companionship of another adult to smooth things out. When one of his family members were around—especially the female ones—he didn't feel quite so inept. Like maybe he could handle being a widower with five rowdy boys. And he liked not having to eat his own cooking. And not being alone.

"I'm hungry," Ivan solemnly intoned.

The rest of the boys jumped in with similar complaints.

"All right. All right." Josias laughed. "Let's go find us some supper."

They filed into the kitchen, Josias and all five boys.

His children gathered around the table while Josias settled Tommy into his high chair and went to the pantry to see what he could find.

There wasn't much. Hadn't he just bought groceries?

"Just a sec," he told his boys, swinging back to the refrigerator. Whether he had recently bought food or not, there wasn't much left today. Apparently, five boys consumed a lot of food, a fact that he hadn't realized when he had so much help around the house.

He scanned the shelves from top to bottom, his gaze

finally snagging on a block of cheese. A sudden memory swamped him: everyone sitting around the table eating tomato soup and grilled cheese sandwiches. Marie was smiling and the children were happily slurping as snow fell outside the windows.

Well, there was no snow, and Marie was gone, but soup and sandwiches sounded like something that he could do.

He grabbed the block of cheese, then made his way back over to the pantry.

"Dat, are you cooking?"

He turned to find all his boys watching him carefully. Eli and Harley even had their mouths hanging open. At least Tommy was doing his own thing, slapping his hands against the smooth flat service of the tray in front of him, unaware of the drama about to unfold. So, Josias wasn't much for kitchen duty. But what choice did he have?

He decided to play it off. "Of course," he scoffed and turned back to the pantry searching for the familiar red and white cans Marie used to keep on hand for just an emergency. None. Maybe they had changed the cans since he had taken notice, but after a quick scan of labels he surmised that there was no tomato soup, only cans of stewed tomatoes, another emergency provision he supposed since Marie had canned tomatoes half the summer.

Maybe they had some other kind of soup…

"Dat," Ivan said, his tone as serious as Dale's. "Are you going to find us something to eat?"

Josias pasted on a confident look and faced his children. "Of course," he said. "I'm just looking for something really special."

Eli and Harley rubbed their bellies in anticipation.

"Dawdi gave us something special for snack," Dale told him. "But that was ages ago."

"Oh *jah*?" Josias asked absently as he started through the stash of home canned goods. Except that stash had dwindled since Marie had gotten sick—just as the garden was coming in and her health went quickly downhill. One minute she was alive and well and the next it seemed she was gone. At the time he hadn't been worried about canning tomatoes. Or soup. Or anything other than his wife.

His gaze swung back to the cans of tomatoes sitting innocently next to tins of tuna. Marie used to make a *wunderbaar* casserole using the fish, but he thought it needed soup as well. Not tomato, but another kind. Maybe chicken. No, that didn't sound right. No matter.

He reached for the can of tomatoes. How different was tomato soup from tomatoes? There couldn't be much. Maybe spices. He had spices.

He grabbed two cans of stewed tomatoes and turned back toward the stove.

"Is that our special meal?" Harley asked. His blue eyes, so like Josias's own, were hopeful and bright.

"Jah." Once again Josias summoned all his confidence.

But when he opened the can, it didn't look like soup. It looked like a can of tomatoes. Well, two cans of tomatoes with pepper in it. Maybe if he added a little garlic as well.

He did and stirred up the mess. The bits of tomato needed to be smaller, he decided. Tomato soup was sort of smooth. But he had no idea how to make that a reality. It would have to do for now.

He turned the flame down on the stove and switched his attention to the grilled cheese. That he knew a bit more about, though he had never made one himself. Yet how hard could it be?

He grabbed the bread and started buttering both sides.

"That's not how Mamm did it," Eli said, swinging his legs as he waited as patiently as a five-year-old boy could wait.

Of course it wasn't. "These are *my* special grilled cheese sandwiches," he told the boy, hoping his voice sounded confident and a little mysterious. Josias wasn't about to admit to his children that he had no clear idea as to how to make this meal work.

How many sandwiches could he make at one time? Only two, by his calculations, and that was using the big skillet to toast them.

Toast. That was the solution. He might not be able to remember how Marie juggled two sandwiches per batch and five hungry boys, but he could toast bread in the oven.

Josias fetched the large cookie sheet from the drawer under the oven and started loading it with buttered bread.

"*Da-at.* Are you sure you know what you are doing?"

Josias turned to give Harley a flabbergasted look. *"Jah."* At least Tommy didn't think he was messing up at every turn.

After he distributed cheese to all the slices, he loaded the tray into the oven and turned it on. Then he moved his attention back to the soup.

But it didn't really look like soup. It was still too chunky. Oh well, it would have to do. He smashed what he could with the tongs of a fork and called it good. Maybe if he presented the meal like it was supposed to be this way, the kids would eat it without question.

Josias peeked into the oven, where the cheese was beginning to melt but the edges weren't turning brown. Had he done something wrong? Maybe he needed to turn the stove up a bit more.

He raised the temperature fifty degrees, then casually glanced back at the table, where his boys continued to monitor his every move. He wasn't sure they would buy his excuses, but at least they wouldn't go to bed hungry. That had to count for something, *jah*? And tomorrow he would figure out how to make something they would eat. He could roof a house, cut hay and vaccinate his herd. He couldn't be beaten by soup and sandwiches.

Another check on the bread, but still the edges weren't browning. Instead, they seemed to be drying out. Maybe that was just a part of the cooking process. He turned the oven up a few more degrees and went to get the bowls from the cabinet.

"Harley, you and Eli come put out the spoons and saucers." He would serve the soup at the stove.

"Uh, Dat," Dale started hesitantly. "Is there supposed to be smoke?"

A thin gray line of smoke was rising from the top of the oven door.

Josias yanked open the oven door and grabbed a pot holder. The pan was smoldering, but still the edges of the bread weren't toasted around the cheese. Maybe he should have put it on broil…

Gingerly, he set the pan on the stovetop next to the bubbling pot of almost-soup. He lifted the edge of one of the pieces of bread to check underneath. Thankfully, it wasn't completely black. Just overly brown, and he supposed that all the smoke came from the burning butter and not scorching bread. Seems he got them out just in time. At least something was going right in this meal.

He turned and set the pan on the hot pad in the center of the table, careful to keep it out of little Tommy's reach. It wasn't so bad.

"What's that?" Eli asked, his tone skeptical.

"Grilled cheeses," Dale explained.

Eli couldn't take his eyes off the pan in the center of the table. *"Jah?"* He was anything but convinced.

"Dat's special grilled cheeses," Harley added.

Ivan nodded importantly, having to be a part of the conversation.

"*Jah*," Josias said with more confidence than he felt. It was bread and melted cheese. How could that be a bad recipe?

He turned from his boys and started ladling out bowls of soup. In no time he was sitting down with his children to enjoy this meal that he had prepared. That was something, right?

He bowed his head, and the boys followed suit, asking for God's blessing for the food they were about to eat.

He raised his head and picked up his spoon, but the boys remained with their hands folded in their laps.

"What's wrong?" he asked, spoonful of soup halfway between the bowl and his mouth.

"This is soup and grilled cheeses?" Eli asked.

"Eat," Josias demanded. He had done the best he could with what he had on hand. It might not be the way his wife had made it, but it would fill their bellies and hold them until tomorrow.

His sons reluctantly raised their spoons and started to eat. Satisfied, Josias raised his bite of soup to his lips. It wasn't bad. But it was far from good. And it was even further from soup. More like warmed up tomatoes with pepper and garlic.

He took another bite, then dipped his cheese bread into the soup. Not too bad. Again. Not good, but not really bad, either.

Yet he couldn't ignore the skeptical looks on his son's faces. Only Tommy ate with abandon.

It took Josias twice as long to eat supper than it ever had before, but he finally managed to get his boys upstairs and ready for bed. As he lay down himself, only one thought kept circling in his mind.

We can't continue on this way.

Chapter Three

Naomi woke up the following morning still exhausted from the day before. Her cheeks hurt from smiling all day, and her calf muscles ached from running around making sure Mattie and Samuel's wedding was as perfect as it could be. Still, it was worth it. Even with the strange run-in she'd had with Josias Schrock. She could only say a small prayer that he truly hadn't taken offense. That he had been telling the complete truth when he had said that he was ready to go home even before she started saying things she should have never said.

But that was a worry for another time.

Her father and her sisters were already up and dressed by the time Naomi made her way down the stairs. It felt strange to be back in her father's house once more. Itchy, like her skin was too tight. She had been staying with Mattie since David died. She and Evie had immediately gone to help with the children and the goats. But now that Evie was getting married to Freeman Yoder, she had moved back home with the rest of the family. Naomi figured she would be doing the same soon. Permanently. Mattie no longer needed so much help with the kids and her dairy farm and now had a new husband to bond with. There were already three children under foot; a wayward sister would be too much, for sure. Naomi would stay on for a couple of weeks, but after that she would be on her own until—hopefully—she would be accepted to art school.

Then she would have to tell her family her plans. But until that time, she wasn't going to worry about those problems. Today had its own.

"Good morning," Lizzie chirped, shifting patiently as she waited for Naomi to take her seat.

A chorus of greetings went up around the table. Everyone had gathered and was apparently waiting for her to eat their breakfast. At least she had made her way downstairs before they had to call for her.

Naomi slipped into her place at the table and bowed her head for the meal's silent prayer. She opened her eyes and lifted her gaze when she heard her father rustling in his seat.

"Everything looks so good," Naomi said as her father started passing around the platters of food. Sausage, bacon and homemade bread smeared with butter and perfectly toasted.

That was one good thing about being back at home; she wasn't the only one who baked. Sarah Ann had been trying her hand at pies and such ever since she had gone to work at the bakery that their neighbor Suzanne Raber had opened behind her house. Her husband, Daniel, had lost a leg a couple of years back, and Suzanne opened the bakery to help with their living expenses. Suzanne was a whiz in the kitchen, and the bakery was an instant hit.

"This bread is amazing," Naomi said, taking a small bite even as she smeared jam on a piece for Bethann, Mattie's oldest.

Sometimes Naomi wondered how her father did it, keeping his patience around so many females. She had asked him once, and he had just smiled and said each one of them was a blessing, and he was grateful for them all. Yet she knew. Like most men, he had longed for a son. Now he was saddled with a passel of granddaughters as well.

She chanced a quick glance at her father, who was holding baby Davida, Mattie's youngest child. Thomas Ebersol was feeding the baby a bottle, smiling down at her as if she was the most precious thing in the world. Naomi supposed that she was.

"What are we doing today?" Evie asked as she added more butter to her already buttered toast. Evie burned up a lot of energy even though she had been born with a mild case of spina bifida. Or maybe it was because she had. Evie was fiercely independent and always the first in line to volunteer to help with whatever needed help. Naomi knew firsthand that Evie was determined to be her own person and not allow her disabilities to completely define who she wanted to be. Of course, there were times when Evie had to accept that she couldn't do everything. Why, just last month she had tried her best to milk Mattie's herd of goats by herself only to discover that it was more than she could handle alone. Naomi knew that her sister had learned a valuable lesson in accepting limitations, but also to remember that her family was there for her always.

Naomi just hoped her family was with her when she heard back from the art school in Philadelphia.

She had thought Evie's good friend Helen had been out of her mind to run off to Lancaster to see how they lived in their fancy houses and their commercial businesses. But

Philadelphia... That was a completely different world. How would she fare when the time came?

She would be fine, she decided, willing her heart rate to slow as she forked a helping of scrambled eggs onto her plate next to her pile of bacon.

Besides, she hadn't even been accepted yet. They might take one look at the drawings she had sent and pitch them right into the trash. She had no way of gauging if her artwork was any good. Art and self-expression weren't exactly lifted up in her community. In fact, it was downright frowned upon. So, she kept it a secret, from everyone, including her sisters. She felt deep in her heart that most of them would support her. Especially Mattie and Evie, but she knew that her twin would never understand her need to take pencil to paper, sometimes even crayon to paper, and reproduce images and memories in her own way.

"I thought we were going over to Mattie's to help today," Naomi said, forcing herself out of her own thoughts.

"We could have been there to help with the morning milking," Evie said. "But someone slept in."

Naomi felt the heat of embarrassment seep into her cheeks. "Someone let me sleep in." She returned her sister's jovial barb. It was nearly impossible to oversleep with so many people around the house, but Naomi had been exhausted when she had finally gotten into bed the night before. Why no one had bothered to wake her up wasn't her fault. Except she could have set her wind-up alarm. But she hadn't, figuring Bethann would have crawled into bed with her long before the sun came up. Perhaps Bethann had been exhausted as well. After all, it wasn't every day that a girl got a new *dat*.

"We can still go over and make sure they have everything they need," Priscilla put in.

Sarah Ann nodded. "Plus, Mattie will skin us if we don't bring her girls back before lunch."

Everyone laughed. It had taken all of them to convince their sister that she should have at least one night of newly wedded bliss without her children around. Mattie had argued that Bethann wouldn't understand, and Gracie would be confused, and Davida was still too young to take a bottle. None of it came to pass, but just went to prove what a wonderful, loving mother Mattie Ebersol Byler really was.

They ate and discussed what they were going to do once they got to Mattie and Samuel's. It would be weird for a while, adding Samuel's name to the description of the house that had for nearly a year been just Mattie's, but Naomi knew that she would get used to it with time.

After breakfast was eaten and the dishes washed and put away, Evie and Sarah Ann gathered up their nieces, Priscilla grabbed her twins, and Naomi went down into the basement to check for any leftover food they might have from the wedding. Anything remaining she would divide up between the two households, despite how long the wedding had lasted. Still, there should be a little bit of cake…

There was actually plenty of cake left. She counted three…no, four of the paper boxes they had used to store it. Mixed in with three aluminum pie containers. If nothing else, they would have dessert.

"Lizzie," Naomi called. She would need help getting all this up the stairs.

As she waited for her sister to respond, she looked around the basement to see if there was a cardboard box she could use to transport at least part of the find to Mattie's house.

Thankfully, there was one sitting off in one corner, atop a large, unfamiliar cooler. Yesterday, Naomi had been in charge of the food, and she didn't remember that ice chest at all. Perhaps one of her aunts brought it and told another of her sisters about it. It was the only explanation she had. Or maybe it was just an ice chest that had gotten pushed off into one corner and forgotten about long ago.

She grabbed the handle and pulled, instantly realizing that it was full of something.

"What is it?" Lizzie called back from the top of the stairs.

"I don't know," Naomi absently replied, looking at the ice chest with amazement.

"If you don't know, why did you call me?" Lizzie shot back.

Naomi shook her head even though her sister couldn't see her. "I want you to grab some cake and—oh, get down here. I need your help."

Lizzie didn't answer, but Naomi could hear the patter of her feet against the wooden steps. "What is it?" she asked, coming into view.

"I'm not sure." Only one way to find out. She flipped the lid up on the cooler. Inside, stacked neatly, one on top of the other, two stacks side by side, were six untouched disposable aluminum pans of…something.

Yet the herby smell was unmistakable.

"Chicken and filling," she and Lizzie said at the same time.

"But where did it come from?" Lizzie asked.

Naomi almost pointed to the corner of the basement

when it clicked what her sister was truly asking. "I don't know…maybe Janie?"

Janie Ebersol was their aunt, married to their father's brother, Karl. Karl was Thomas's only brother and only sibling who lived in Millers Creek.

Lizzie shut the lid and pulled the cooler away from Naomi's shins. Sure enough, Karl Ebersol was written in neat block letters across the back side. She shot Naomi a look, then laid a hand on top of one of the pans. "It's still cool."

Naomi shook her head. "We really could have used this yesterday," she said. Then again, letting everyone know that there was no food remaining had spurred the straggling guests into leaving. It might have been a blessing in disguise.

"What do we do with it now?" Lizzie closed the lid once more. "I mean, besides taking it upstairs."

"Looks like we're having chicken and filling when we get to Mattie's."

But still there would be a lot left over. Too much for the Ebersols to get through before everyone was sick of eating wedding food.

Then out of the blue, Josias Schrock's face appeared in her mind's eye. He was on his own since his mother and sister had gone to the western half of the state. But she couldn't lead with that, not without taking a teasing from her sister.

"Didn't Helen and her *mamm* go to New Wilmington?" She did her best to make her voice sound offhanded as if she really didn't quite remember.

"*Jah*…and?" Then Lizzie dipped her chin in acknowledgment. "You think we should take some over to Elmer and Levi?" Josias's father and brother.

"It would help Esther." She knew his sister had to be working overtime trying to take care of the two men by herself.

"Okay, but that's still a lot." Lizzie cast a skeptical glance at the cooler.

"Josias!" Naomi said his name as if she had just thought about it. At least she hoped that was how her voice sounded. Or else her sister would start to tease her. Even though Naomi had told her several times that she had no interest in dating anyone from their district. Their community even. Having a life just like her sisters was not something she had listed in her goals. It was merely an imaginary list, all in her brain, because if someone found it, how would she explain her desire to go away to art school?

"Good plan." Lizzie smiled as Naomi breathed a small, very small, sigh of relief. She had avoided the razzing. At least for now.

"So, you take one by Elmer's, and I'll take one by Josias's." It wasn't that she just wanted to see him to see him. She wanted to apologize again for yesterday. He might have been ready to leave before her terrible comment, but it was still a terrible comment that he wasn't supposed to hear. Now if she showed up with food and a smile, surely all would be forgiven and eventually—hopefully sooner rather than later—forgotten.

Her sister shrugged. "Sounds good to me."

Naomi shifted the pan of food and braced it against her side, holding it with one hand. The other she raised to knock on the door to Josias's home. The door was painted blue, and the color took her aback. She smiled and knocked again.

It was something of a local myth that the Amish families in the area would paint their front door blue if a woman of marriageable age lived there. Seeing as how Josias was a man and the father of five boys, well, that proved that theory wrong. She knew that there was something in the air that caused the people in the area to favor the color blue. Just a small phenomenon and not a thing more.

She supposed one could argue that Josias was a widower and still very eligible. Though very much a man.

She put a stop to that thought. He was a good Amish man. A handsome Amish man. But she was not in the market for a romance. Not when every day she checked the mail for a letter from Philadelphia. Maybe once she came back from art school. Maybe then she could think about such matters as weddings and marriages. But there was a part of her that wondered if she even *would* come back. She would be shunned, and she would have to go through the process of getting reinstated into the church. She didn't see why that wouldn't happen for her, though—she was getting ahead of herself. She hadn't even left yet. Hadn't even been accepted into the school.

Suddenly a scream sounded, high-pitched and long followed by anguished wailing. But it wasn't coming from inside the house. It seemed to be coming from around back.

Naomi wasted no time. She hopped off the porch and ran around the house.

Then she stopped in her tracks.

Josias was bending down to pick up his youngest boy.

Thomas, maybe. No, Tommy. It was close enough to her father's name that she could remember it. Though as she looked around at the other children, she couldn't think of even one of their names. They were jumping around, all talking at once, each one apparently telling their side of what happened to their brother.

What appeared to be a bedsheet was strewn across the yard in a fresh puddle of mud courtesy of last night's rain. The children stepped on it, not heeding its very existence.

Other pieces of clothing and whatnot floated on the small breeze, anchored to the laundry line stretched across the yard behind him.

"Shhh..." Josias crooned. "You're okay."

Tommy threw his head back and continued to howl as if he had suffered the greatest indignity.

Naomi gave a fleeting thought to turning around and leaving the food on the front porch with a note that it was from her...er, Mattie's wedding. But in that next instant, Josias looked up and caught her gaze.

He cleared his throat, turned a lovely shade of pink and set his crying son on his feet. Tommy immediately fell to his knees once more. Josias started toward her.

The boys noticed that their father was looking at something else entirely and so turned their attention to her as well. They ran ahead of him, rushing up to see what she had brought. Of course, in their excitement, they all began to talk at once.

"Hold up," Naomi said. She gave a shrill whistle, and the boys fell silent. "One at a time. You." She pointed to the tallest. "Go first."

"What are you doing here?"

"Bringing you some food."

Just then Josias strolled up. Tommy was still behind him, crying. Naomi wondered why he wasn't consoling the boy, but really it was none of her business. Instead, she pointed to the second boy in line.

"What kind of food?"

"Chicken and filling."

"Yum," he said, rubbing his tummy in anticipation.

She pointed to the boy next to him. "Your turn."

He was the smallest of the four, and she had a feeling he was the youngest as well. He shuffled in place and looked at his feet before finally asking, "Why are you here?"

Hadn't she already answered that question? No mind. She could answer it again as long as they weren't all talking at once. "I brought your family a pan of chicken and filling that was leftover from my sister's wedding."

"Oh." His eyes were huge, the palest blue she had ever seen. They made her think of a puppy she had seen once. A husky she believed the breed was. Beautiful. Beautiful dog. Beautiful eyes. Handsome boy.

"And you?" She pointed to the final child.

"Who are you?"

Naomi couldn't stop her laughter. She supposed of all the questions that might be the best one of all.

"She's Naomi Ebersol," Josias said. They turned in unison to stare at their father. "She goes to church with us," he explained.

That seemed to be enough for the boys, and they filed off, back to whatever game they had been playing before she had arrived on the scene.

Tommy had finally stopped crying and had rejoined his

brothers in a log fort that had been built on the opposite side of the yard.

"Hi," Josias said. "I didn't expect to see you today."

She nodded, suddenly feeling self-conscious at her plan to bring him food to bribe him into forgetting what she had said the day before. More than anything, she wouldn't want those words to get back to her sister Mattie, who might have hurt feelings over her mistake. It just wasn't worth it. Plus, it was something she should have never said, no matter how tired she was.

"I came with a peace offering." That sounded better than bribe.

"I heard. *Danki*." He smiled, and his entire face seemed relaxed for the first time since she had arrived.

She held the pan toward him.

He awkwardly took it as if it might bite him at any moment. "If this is about yesterday—" he started.

"About yesterday—" she said at the same time.

They both chuckled uncomfortably.

"You first," he said with a nod.

"I just wanted to ask you not to—" But that was as far as she got before she noticed that he was wearing some kind of apron. It was a crocheted piece that looked a little like the ones the servers wore in the Mexican restaurant in town. Wide, but shallow pockets on both sides, with a tie around the back. But instead of an order pad and pens, this one was stuffed with...clothespins.

"Are you doing laundry?" she asked, tilting her head to one side as if daring him to not tell her the truth.

"Well, it's—" he started. Then he shook his head. "I know it's Sunday, but there just aren't enough hours in a week. And now with Mamm and Helen gone… Well, Esther is spending more time at home with Dat and Levi…"

"Leaving you to fend for yourself," Naomi finished for him.

"Jah." He pressed his lips together in a grim smile. "Something like that."

Perfect. And just the leverage she needed.

"Okay then, Josias Schrock, rule breaker, you don't tell anyone what I said yesterday at the wedding, and I won't tell anyone that you're doing work on the Lord's Day."

"Deal." He stretched out his right hand, but before she could shake it, another wail started behind him. It was more of a keening at first, gradually growing louder until it reached a crescendo pitch that was sure to leave them all deaf.

"He needs a nap." Josias had to yell over his son's crying in order to be heard.

"Apparently," Naomi hollered in return. She resisted the urge to stick her fingers into her ears to try to block out some of the shrill noise.

Josias turned and made his way over to his son, lifting him into his arms once more.

"Should you lay him down?" Naomi asked. She wasn't one to tell another how to run their life. After all, she didn't want anyone telling her how to run hers. But for some reason she thought that Josias Schrock needed a little help in that area.

"Every time I try, he wakes up again. And I needed to get the laundry hung out. So here we are."

She hesitated but only for a moment. "Get him inside," she said. "I'll take care of the clothes."

It only took a minute to remove the apron from around his middle.

"I have one for gathering eggs, too," he explained as she tied it around herself.

"Of course you do. Now shoo." She motioned him toward the house. He only paused for a moment, then carried the squalling Tommy inside.

"Come on, boys," she said to the remainder of the Schrocks. "Let's do this."

"What?" The tallest boy was the one who spoke, and she figured once again that he was the oldest. Though he wasn't that much taller than the next boy.

"What's your name?" she asked him.

"Eli," the blond-haired boy chirped.

"Are you the oldest?"

He shook his head and jerked his thumb toward the taller dark-haired boy standing next to him. "No. Dale is."

"And you're Dale?" she asked just to be certain. The second tallest of Josias's boys nodded. He had dark brown hair like his father and pale blue eyes like his littlest brother.

"Good. Okay then, Eli, you go over there and get me that milk crate." She pointed to where several lay up against the side of the barn. "In fact, get two of them."

He nodded enthusiastically, then headed off to do the chore.

"Now, Dale, this is how this is going to work."

By then, Eli had returned with the milk crates.

She showed him where to place them, then set the basket of clothes in between the twin clotheslines.

"Now you." She pointed to the other brown-haired cutie.

"Harley," he answered.

"You, Harley, are going to stand here, and you—"

"His name is Ivan."

"Okay, Ivan, you stand over here." She placed the two smaller boys next to the milk crates.

"What are we doing?" Dale asked. He was a quiet thing. Soft-spoken and nearly timid.

"We are learning how to hang the laundry."

Eli scoffed. "That's woman's work."

Naomi pulled a face. "It is until you don't have any clean clothes. And since these are your things, you are going to help care for them."

She thought he might argue, but she gave a stern look, and he must have decided that it wasn't worth it. Instead, he shrugged and climbed up onto the milk crate in front of his brother.

In no time at all, with all four boys helping and with a little assistance from her, the laundry was hung to dry. The soiled bedsheet was pulled from the mud and wrapped up in the basket for when Josias or whoever did the laundry again.

She was walking it over to the back porch to leave it for the man of the house, when he came easing out the screen door.

"What happened?" he asked.

She started taking off the apron.

"We hung out the clothes," Harley said, bouncing on his toes. He seemed more than excited that he had learned a new chore today.

"I thought it was woman's work, but Naomi said no. It wasn't." Eli grinned as if he had the wisdom of the elders.

Josias stared at the laundry then looked at his smiling boys, then back to Naomi. "You did all this?" he asked.

She wrinkled her forehead into a frown. "Uh...*jah*."

"While I was in the house?" he asked.

"Yes."

"While I was inside, you got my boys to work together and hang up laundry?"

She nodded, unsure of where he was going with this. "Yes." The word was hesitant.

"I need a nanny," he said on a rush. "I'll pay you. Room and board, whatever it is you need. But I have to have some help right now, and you'd be perfect for the job."

Surely he wasn't serious.

"*Danki* for the compliment. The food is on the back porch." She turned to leave, and he stopped her, placing his fingers on her upper arm.

"Naomi, please," he said, his voice taking on an urgency that had her shifting in place. "I really need some help, and I would like to hire you."

Apparently, he *was* serious. Or he had seriously lost his mind. At any rate, his boys seemed well-behaved enough. It wasn't like they would be hard to look after, but she wasn't in the market for a long-term job. She was still planning on moving back in with Mattie and Samuel and helping out with the goats until she heard from the art school. Not that she was guaranteed a place in this fall's class. How did one remain humble and stay positive at the same time? But hopefully really soon, she would be packing her things for Philadelphia. She needed to cut Josias's idea off at the root, lest he decide to go to her father with it.

"*Danki*, but no," she said firmly with a stern shake of her head, then turned and marched around the house and back to her buggy.

He stopped her just before she could hoist herself into the carriage seat. "Please," he said again, laying one hand on her arm to stop her. "Just hear me out."

She should tell him no. She should tell him that she had plans. She didn't have to tell him what those plans were or that they didn't include playing teacher/nursemaid to a bunch of rowdy boys. But there was something in his eyes…a softness, a quiet understanding, a hint of pleading mixed with a great deal of desperation. Or maybe it was something else entirely. No matter. She should tell him no, and yet she found herself saying, "You have five minutes."

Chapter Four

Josias's mind went blank. He had five minutes to convince Naomi to help him take care of his children this summer. She had to be at loose ends since her sister just got married. And it seemed as if God put her here today to help him. Josias didn't necessarily believe in signs, but he would sure enough accept this as one. Plus, she was truly amazing if she could get his brood working together only minutes after meeting them.

"I'll pay you." That had to be the worst reason to lead with.

"I'm not a nanny," she said plainly.

"You should be," he replied. "You're great with kids." He should have realized this earlier with the number of nieces she had, and it only made him more determined to have her as his summer support.

She shrugged. "I help my sister some. But the secret is to listen to them."

Listen to them? How did listening to them get meals prepared and baths taken and everything else that needed to be done that seemed to eat up day after day? Every day seemed shorter and shorter while he grew more and more exhausted. "I'm not sure that's the answer."

She shook her head and swung up into her buggy. "Maybe not," she said. "But I can't help you."

"Do you have a sister, maybe?" He was certain she did, but there were enough Ebersol girls running around Millers Creek that he couldn't keep up with who belonged to whom.

"I do, but they all have jobs." She gathered up the reins, and he knew his five minutes were ticking away faster than his brain was looking for the reason she should help him.

"Will you ask them?" He hated the desperate edge to his voice. He wasn't desperate. He was merely in need. "A friend even."

"Okay," she said. "No promises, but I'll ask around."

The next morning Josias made his way out to the barn, her final words still ringing in his ears. Naomi would be perfect as a summer nanny for his brood, but if she wouldn't accept the position maybe she could help him find someone who would.

This morning his internal alarm had gone off five minutes before his clock, and he had gone downstairs and grabbed a cold biscuit while he waited for the coffee to brew. Soon he would have Dale helping him, but right now, Josias needed his oldest inside with the other boys. That was the most important thing. Josias could sling food for the cows and get them all milked by himself—what he couldn't do was take care of a toddler while he was doing so. But he knew the time was coming.

Last night he had taken a few minutes and cleared his thoughts. He closed his eyes and tried his best to remember the names of the young women in the community who didn't have jobs or worked outside their homes. Yet he found himself solely devising ways to convince Naomi to accept his offer. It was only for the summer. Only until his mother and sister came back from New Wilmington. If his sister did indeed return. That was something no one in the family seemed to be prepared to talk about. Since Josias had his own problems, he didn't press the matter.

He knew that most people in the district would just tell him to get married, but he had been a terrible husband. He couldn't help his wife when she needed him the most. He had failed her, and he couldn't put another in the same situation. It wasn't fair, but there it was. The awful truth.

After milking the cows, storing the milk and turning the heifers back out into the pasture, Josias made his way into the house. The boys were just starting to wake up, all in their typical way. The oldest four were rubbing their eyes and yawning while Tommy was running circles around them, chasing a cat that someone had allowed in while Josias was out in the barn.

"Dale, please get that cat out of here," Josias commanded, realizing as he said the words that everything seemed to fall on Dale. As the oldest, he was the best one for a lot of the chores, but it wasn't equal in distribution.

"*Jah*, Dat," Dale sleepily replied and started chasing behind Tommy, who was still chasing the cat.

Josias sighed and made his way back to the door. "Chase him this way," he ordered, hoping his plan would work. The boys chased the cat toward Josias, who opened the door to allow his escape. Once the tabby was safely outside, Tommy sat down hard on his rump, threw his little head back and wailed.

Josias scooped him up and tried to comfort him, though he was certain his own hearing would never be the same.

"He's upset about the cat being put outside," Eli stated helpfully.

"I believe you're right," Josias said, patting his youngest on the back and shushing him the same way he had seen Marie do to the boys countless times. But Tommy wasn't having it. "Kitty. Kitty. Kitty," he cried.

"See?" Eli said as Harley and Ivan nodded in unison.

"Should I let it back in?" Dale asked, starting for the door.

Josias stuck out one hand to stop his son's progress. There was enough chaos without adding the cat back into the mix, and once Josias started cooking breakfast, all bets were off.

It seemed to take forever, but Tommy's cries slowly turned to sad little hiccups, and he laid his head down on Josias's shoulder. "Kitty," he mumbled sleepily and settled in as if to take an early morning nap.

Great. Josias had managed to calm him, but he knew from previous experience that if he tried to lay the toddler down, he would wake up and the cries would begin anew.

"Dale, can you and Eli get the food out of the refrigerator?"

"What food?" Eli wanted to know.

Josias would like the answer to that one, too. He made his way to the fridge and pulled the door open. Eggs and bacon and maybe some toast, but that would all require two hands or more help than a five-year-old and a six-year-old could contribute. Then he spotted the pan containing the chicken and filling that Naomi Ebersol had brought the day before.

So, it wasn't breakfast food, but it would fill all their bellies and get them started on their day. "Forgive me, Marie," he murmured and instructed the boys to pull the pan off the shelf and place it in the cold oven. It and the food could heat up at the same time.

"That's our breakfast?" Eli asked, wrinkling his nose in distaste. Or maybe it was confusion.

"Of course." Josias hoped his voice sounded confident.

Tommy released a small sigh and snuggled a little deeper into the crook of Josias's shoulder. Poor baby. He hadn't been sleeping well, waking up in the middle of the night inconsolable. Which meant Josias spent half the night attempting to comfort him before he fell back into a fitful sleep.

"That's supper food," Dale added.

Josias shook his head and held on to his certainty. "We've had breakfast food for supper, *jah*?"

His boys nodded vigorously.

"Okay, then, this is supper food for breakfast."

"If you say so," Dale said, clearly skeptical.

But what choice did he really have? He couldn't disturb Tommy any more than he could learn how to make eggs that weren't rubbery in the time that he was allowed. So, this would do for now.

The boys ate heartily enough. One thing Josias could say about the Ebersol women: they could cook. The chicken and filling was delicious if not an odd breakfast choice, but bellies were filled and the day continued.

"Let's go," he called, thankful that this was the last week

of school for Dale. Of course, there was the end of school picnic coming up on Friday, but that was not something to worry about today.

His boys tromped out the door, and Josias shut it behind him as they made their way to the road.

"John-John Peight gets to walk to school by himself," Dale grumbled as they started toward the one-room schoolhouse just about a half a mile away. It was the standard conversation for the morning walk.

"John-John Peight is eight." *And not my child*, he wanted to add but somehow refrained. *Jah*, he was probably being a little overprotective walking Dale to school every morning, especially seeing as how it got everyone out of the house to trek down the road, but Josias needed to know that his son got to school all right. He could only chalk his worry up to losing Marie so close to the beginning of the school year. Now here they were, almost at the last day, and he still hadn't learned to let go.

"Next year you can walk by yourself…maybe," he quickly added.

"Next year Eli will be in school, too."

He hadn't thought about that. His kids were growing up so fast. Too fast. Marie wasn't here to watch them, and he felt as if his worry was eating up more time than the simple passage of days. Where had it all gone?

Soon they would mark the year anniversary of Marie's death, the typical mourning period taken by most who lost a spouse. But he had no desire to remarry. Which made his job offer to Naomi Ebersol all the more important. But why wouldn't she accept it? It was almost as if she knew something about him that he didn't even know himself.

"Beth Byler walks to school by herself," Dale countered.

"I am sure that Beth walks to school with her brother Joshie," Josias replied. "Listen, there are four days left in school. Let's keep it as it is for now. Then when school starts back in August, we'll talk about it some more, okay?" That seemed to satisfy Dale for the time being. And Josias supposed that having two children walk to school together should be a relief to his father's mind, but the thought just made him feel even sicker in the stomach than the thought of Dale walking by himself. How do these other parents do it? He supposed that they hadn't lost the way he had. That they weren't lacking the way he was.

Maybe he was going about this the wrong way. Maybe he needed a strapping young man to help him. But that just made him wish that his brother Elam was there. He could use his brother's help, but he had a feeling that if Elam hadn't gone on *rumspringa* and never come back, his brother would most likely be helping their father and Levi on the family farm. But as it was, his brother was gone. Josias had married young, moved out and had a passel of kids. Now that his wife was gone, he was struggling.

The schoolyard was full of kids running, playing tag and expending energy, and he was sure their teacher was grateful they got rid of it before the start of the day. She was on the porch of the schoolhouse preparing to ring the bell to let the children know it was time for class to begin. Beside her stood Naomi Ebersol. That was when he remembered that Lizzie Ebersol was Naomi's sister, and Lizzie was the schoolteacher. It seemed like everywhere he turned Naomi was there. And he couldn't help but believe that maybe it truly was some sort of sign.

He felt a tug on his pant leg. He looked down to see Harley gazing up at him, an expectant light in his gray-blue eyes.

Josias smiled down at his son. "Go ahead. You can play for a minute, and then we've got to go home." He barely got the entire sentence out before his boys all ran for the playground. Even Tommy had broken free and was toddling behind his brothers. Josias resisted the urge to run after his youngest. His brothers would watch out for him, though that was something Josias had to remind himself of constantly. But it was a fact he knew would always remain.

He gave one last look to his children and started up the porch steps to where Lizzie and Naomi stood. He should use this opportunity to his advantage. If it were a sign, and indeed he thought it was, he should use the opportunity to state his cause.

Okay, so he knew she was really there to talk to her sister, maybe help her with the lessons today. But why today of all days?

"Good morning," Lizzie said with a sweet smile. Like her sister Naomi, Lizzie had beautiful sea-colored eyes. Truly like nothing he had ever seen. Though where Lizzie's were open and welcoming, Naomi's held hidden secrets. Perhaps that was why she turned down his job offer.

"Good morning." He nodded at each woman in turn.

A heartbeat passed with him still trying to figure out how to broach the subject. He thought perhaps he might ease into it, start some other conversation and then casually ask Naomi once again if she would be interested in being his nanny while Helen was gone. But he just couldn't find the words that seemed slick enough to bring up the subject without her knowing immediately what he was doing. He vetoed that idea and went for the direct approach.

"So, Naomi," he started. "Did you give any more thought to my job offer?"

"Job offer?" Lizzie looked from one of them to the other.

"I wasn't considering your job offer," Naomi replied. "I seem to remember telling you that I didn't want to accept your job offer."

"Job offer?" Lizzie asked again.

"Well, I just figured you had the night to sleep on it and maybe perhaps you were going to change your mind?"

"Why would I change my mind?"

"What job offer?"

Naomi turned to her sister. "Josias needs a nanny."

"Just until Mamm and Helen get back." Though he wondered when Helen would be coming back. Surely his *mamm* wouldn't be gone longer than the summer. That was what he was counting on anyway.

"Are you interested?" He looked at Lizzie.

She shook her head. "No, I've already promised I'll help Dat in the fields this year."

Josias nodded. It wasn't uncommon to see the women in the valley out working in the fields. When a man like Thomas Ebersol had nothing but daughters, what choice did he have?

"Naomi was just so good with my children," Josias started.

Lizzie turned back to her sister. "When were you—"

"Yesterday, when I took over the chicken and filling we found after the wedding."

"It's just for the summer," Josias said again. "A temporary position."

"I appreciate the offer," Naomi said. "I do, but I've prior commitments for the summer."

"Prior commitments?" he parroted.

"You do?" Lizzie asked, her mouth slightly agape.

Naomi frowned at them both. "*Jah*," she said, directing the word toward him. "I have prior commitments." The last part she slung at her sister.

"How about another sister?"

"Well," Lizzie said, her tone amused. "Mattie is busy with her own family, and Evie is planning her wedding. Priscilla has the twins. I promised to help Dat, and Sarah Ann's working at the Raber's bakery." The Ebersol girls shared a look, then turned back to him, both shaking their heads in near unison. "Sorry," Lizzie said. "I don't think any of us will be able to help."

Chapter Five

By Wednesday afternoon Naomi had finally convinced Lizzie to stop asking questions about her "prior commitments." It wasn't like she could tell her what they were. Because there were none other than worrying about whether or not she would be accepted into art school. No one in her family knew that she had even applied to the school in Philadelphia. As far as Naomi was concerned there was no sense telling them anything about it now. Not yet. She hadn't been accepted. Her telling them that she had been accepted to art school would come with a whole slew of questions including how she managed to get her GED without anyone in the family knowing.

It had been easy, really. It had only taken her a couple of years of studying to complete. But she couldn't go to the Moore College of Art & Design without a high school diploma equivalent. *Jah*, there was going to be a lot of discussion when the time came. If it ever did.

She wasn't sure her drawings were good enough to get her into art school. Only that something in her heart compelled her to take pencil to paper and create and re-create the beauty in front of her. She didn't know what she would do when she finished art school. It was just something she felt obliged to do.

"Still not sure on the color," Evie was saying as they made their way toward the post office. It was a beautiful sunshiny day, with a blue sky only late May in Central Pennsylvania could produce. Soon she knew it would be hot, hotter than any of them enjoyed, but for now the breeze was light and the sun was bright, and the "prior commitments" hadn't crowded in.

"Have you been to the fabric store to look yet?"

Evie sighed. "Four times. Faith even said she would try to order me something new and unusual, but considering how everyone in the valley has been getting married in blue for a hundred years, I'm not sure there *is* new or unusual."

"Why does it have to be unusual?" Naomi asked. They were Amish after all, and their culture was all about conformity. Yet she knew there was that piece of them all that strived for just a little bit of individuality. Not much, but enough to say *I'm a unique creature of God*.

Evie waited for Naomi to open the door to the post office before making her way inside, her aluminum crutches clanging against the tile floor. Despite having been born with spina bifida, Evie was still one of the bravest people that Naomi had ever met. She didn't see her crutches as a weakness, and sometimes such bravery worked against her. But Naomi was so proud of her sister. And now that she had found love with Freeman Yoder, the blessings were more than profound.

"I just don't want it to be the same color that everybody else uses in the same wedding season." Evie turned and waited for Naomi to enter the post office.

Naomi gave a quick nod. "Fair enough. But you know what? I think more than unique and unusual, you should pick something that you like. That you and Freeman like. A color that when you put it on, you'll feel like a bride."

Evie's thoughtful expression melted into a sweet smile of thankfulness. "That's the best thing anyone has said to me since I started planning this wedding."

She moved in to hug Naomi, and Naomi wrapped her arms around her sister. If and when she got into art school and if and when she went to Philadelphia, she was going miss her sisters terribly.

"I still can't believe you're mailing dishcloths," Naomi said. "Didn't that stop like two decades ago?"

Evie shot her a sad smile. "Everybody needs dish towels. And how fun is it to get them in the mail."

How fun. Maybe that was what Naomi needed: a little more excitement in her life. How could dishcloths be fun to get in the mail? What did that say about their lives if looking forward to dishcloths to come in the mail was the thing that gave them joy?

The pair of them got in line and waited their turn, chatting about this and that as the line began to dwindle. Behind her, Naomi heard the bell on the door of the post office ring and knew someone else had come inside. Someone she was fairly certain wasn't mailing dishcloths to a cousin in Ohio who would turn around and mail them to someone in Indiana and so forth until a new group of them finally made their way back to Evie in Millers Creek.

Once it was Evie's turn, she stepped forward, reaching in her bag to pull out the package containing the dishcloths for the dishcloths circle someone in Wisconsin had started.

"I need to mail this," Evie said, setting the box on the counter where the postman could get it.

The worker, whose name was Barney, nodded at them both. They had seen him countless times in the post office and around town. After all, Millers Creek was not that big.

He started punching information into his computer, then turned back to look at Naomi. "Naomi," he said. "Have you checked your post office box today?"

She shook her head, not really surprised that he remembered her name. She had been checking her post office box on a weekly basis for the last three years. But it was a post office box that no one in her family knew she had.

"You have a post office box here?" Evie asked, a frown of confusion puckering her brow.

Naomi shrugged as if it were no big deal. "*Jah*, I've had it for a little while."

"Why?"

Naomi decided it was better to just ignore her sister's question and instead turned to Barney the postman. "I haven't," she said. "Do I need to?"

He shook his head. "You have a certified letter. But I can get it for you without the notification from your box."

A certified letter?

"A certified letter?" Evie echoed Naomi's own thoughts. But Naomi remained silent. Still her heart began to beat a little faster in her chest. It had to be from the art school. There didn't seem to be any way around it. Who else would send her certified mail? But if it *was* from the art school, how was she supposed to keep it hidden from her sister?

There was no way. She couldn't very well tell Barney to just leave it in her box and she would come back later.

That would raise even more questions than if she accepted it outright.

"Give me a second here to finish this up and I'll get it for you, okay?"

Naomi nodded and swallowed hard, her mouth dry.

"You have a post office box and a certified letter?" Evie had turned to stare at her, but Naomi had no answers. At least none that she could give at the moment.

Barney finished shipping off Evie's dishcloths and rapped his knuckles once against the counter. "I'll be right back with that letter."

Naomi pretended to stare at the poster containing the new designs for postage stamps for the year while Evie studied her without blinking. She knew her sister wanted an answer, but it wasn't something she could do. Not right now. Not yet. Not yet.

All too quickly, Barney was back with the letter.

Naomi's hands shook as she signed for it. It was from the college.

As they turned to exit the line, Naomi saw who had come into the post office behind them. None other than Josias Schrock. How was it that every time she seemed to turn around these days he was there? What was that about a bad penny? But she couldn't say he was bad. In fact, he was kind and handsome and godly and had a bunch of other really good qualities that if she were looking for a boss would be great. But she wasn't looking for a job, and the letter in her hands was the exact reason why.

It's a letter to tell me that I haven't been accepted. It's a letter to tell me that I haven't been accepted. It's a letter to tell me that I haven't been accepted.

Maybe if she told herself that enough times, she would believe it. Then it wouldn't sting so badly when she opened the letter and saw the words there in black and white.

They weren't even to the door when Evie turned and stopped her. "Aren't you going to open it?"

No! Naomi wanted to shout. But how derailed would that make her look? She got a certified letter, signed for it, and she wasn't going to open it?

"I thought I would wait until we get home." When she could crawl up in the loft in the barn by herself and read the words without her family watching. It wasn't supposed to happen this way, with her sister studying her every move.

"Open your mail," Evie said, her voice filled with urgent expectancy.

Naomi couldn't think of a single reason why she shouldn't open it. It was certified, and Evie understood as well as she did that certified meant important. Who held on to important mail without opening it?

She tore the end off the envelope. Her hands were shaking even worse now than they had been when she signed for it, but somehow she managed to get it open. She blew in the end of the envelope to widen the sides and pulled the paper from inside. Part of her wanted to just crumple it up and toss it in the trash because she didn't want to read those words. *Thank you, Miss Ebersol, but your application has been denied.* Or whatever it was they would say to her to let her know that she would not be attending their school.

While she stared at the tri-folded piece of paper, her sister slipped the envelope from her fingers. "Moore College of Art & Design?"

Naomi could feel Evie's gaze land on her. She could almost see the questions dancing in the air between them, but she didn't have those answers yet. She didn't have words to explain. She summoned all the courage she had and opened the letter.

Dear Miss Ebersol, we are pleased to inform you—

She did it.
She got in.
She read the opening paragraph again and again even as she knew her sister was staring at her, trying to decipher the meaning behind all this.

"Why is a college of art and design sending you a letter?" Evie asked. Her voice was small, the question barely an inquiry. They both knew why, though Evie had no prior inkling of her plans. Naomi had never shared her drawings with her family. No one had the smallest inkling that she had even considered going away to art school. In their community, it was practically unthinkable.

"I... I applied," Naomi said.

"But you're not going." Evie shook her head and looked up from the telling envelope. "I mean, you can't go. You joined the church. You'll be shunned."

Naomi knew all this. She didn't need reminding of it. But what if she went for a couple of years and then came back? She could say her prayers and ask for forgiveness and earn her way back into the community. Where was the bad in that?

The thought crossed her mind even as she knew what was wrong with it. The outside world was a dangerous place. Sin was a slippery slope. Once she was away from the support of her family and community…well, who would be there to protect her then?

"I—" She didn't know what to say. She wanted to tell her sister that of course she wasn't going. But that wasn't the truth. This had been something that she had been thinking about for years. For years she had looked at this college and studied its programs. She knew by heart what she would need to have to go there and study art. If only they would let her in. Now that dream had become a reality. She was in. But could she go? Could she leave her family behind? That was the real question.

"Naomi, please tell me that you're not leaving to go to art school." Her words were so quietly spoken that Naomi wondered for a moment if she had even said them. But she had, and Evie was waiting for her answer.

Naomi felt as if she had completely lost her powers of speech.

"Of course not."

She whirled around as Josias Schrock sidled up close.

Evie almost melted with relief. "She's not?"

Why was it when a man stepped up everyone tended to listen? She hated that part of the community, but now she was grateful that Josias was keeping her sister's questions at bay.

"Of course not," Josias said. "Because she's engaged to me."

Josias could feel Naomi shaking beside him. He would like to think that she was trembling with gratitude, but he had a feeling the emotion was more akin to anger. He didn't know what made him step forward and try to rescue her from the situation with her sister, but he had. He didn't know why he couldn't come up with a better excuse other than they were engaged, but he hadn't. That was going to lead to all sorts of complications. Especially where his own kids were concerned if they were to ever find out. Hopefully, they wouldn't. Because this engagement was probably going to last about two minutes before Naomi found whatever excuse she needed to tell her sister why she had applied to an art school in Philadelphia.

Suddenly, Josias understood the secrets that he saw in Naomi's eyes. With a sinking feeling in his heart, he realized how much she was like his Marie. He hadn't seen it at first, but he recognized it now. Naomi was restless. Her eyes held a faraway look, as if she were checking the horizon to see what was coming next. He had hoped that when he and Marie had gotten married she would outgrow that desire to see more, do more, have more than their little Amish community could provide.

He pushed the thought away. Marie was gone, and Naomi was still here, most likely ready to tell him off and good.

"Engaged?" Evie's hazel eyes widened with surprise and happiness. He never seen such joy come off a person so quickly as it did off Evie Ebersol in that moment. But he knew the reason. Evie was engaged herself, and once a person fell in love it seemed their sole purpose was to make sure everyone around them was in love as well. And she, Evie, was delighted that Naomi had found love, too.

"Why didn't you say anything?" Evie gushed. "Oh, I know," she continued. "You were just focusing on my joy. You are the sweetest."

So many Amish couples kept their entire engagement a

secret, and with Mattie just now getting married and Evie scheduled to get married in the fall, there was enough good news going around that hers could wait.

"Excuse us?" Naomi said to Evie. It seemed she had found her voice.

She didn't wait for her sister's answer before latching on to Josias's arm and pulling him from the post office. He had no choice but to follow, stumbling along in the wake of her anger.

She marched him out onto the sidewalk before stopping and whirling around to face him. "What are you doing?"

He had almost expected her to yell the words at him, but her voice was eerily quiet for someone whose cheeks were that red with anger. "I thought you could use some help." He smiled at her.

She shook her head. "I don't need that kind of help."

He shrugged. "Okay. Then go back in there and tell her we're not engaged. Then you can explain how you're not going to accept art school in the fall."

She closed her eyes briefly, opened them once again and pinned him with that sea-colored stare. "Maybe I'm not going to art school in the fall."

Josias crossed his arms over his chest and stared down his nose at her. What was the saying? Never kid a kidder. "If you didn't plan on going to that school, you wouldn't have applied."

He knew that one firsthand. Marie had talked constantly about going to school and learning new things, becoming a chef, doing something different other than just being a wife and a mother and a good Amish woman. But she had never taken that final step. It was a regret that he thought she carried with her to the grave. *What ifs* seemed to weigh her down with every year that passed.

"I'm not ready to tell them yet," Naomi said, her voice small.

"Your family?" Josias asked.

She swallowed hard and nodded.

"If you are going, you'll need money," he said. A part of him hated himself for using her dream against her. But if he could get a jump on someone as a nanny for the summer, then perhaps his life would ease up a little bit and things would settle into a new normal that he could handle.

She turned to look at him. "So that's what you think? I should just be your nanny for the summer to make some money?"

"Why not? You work for me for three months, and you'll have cash to take with you. If your family thinks we're engaged, that'll give them time to get used to the idea that you even draw. Because...they don't know, do they?"

He watched the pupils dilate in those big turquoise eyes. There was no hiding the truth. Her family had no clue.

"If they don't even know that you draw and you pull this on them today, what kind of shock would that be?"

She had no answer for him.

"This way they can become accustomed to the idea that you have this hobby at all. And that eventually you want to turn it into something different. Give them the summer, work for me, save your money, and in the fall..." He allowed his voice to trail off.

"In the fall I go to school."

"*Jah*," he said the word, but it was choked. He hated the thought of her leaving their community. Just as he hated the thought of Marie having dreams beyond the valley. He hadn't seen much of what was out there, but he didn't trust it. Yet he knew that unfulfilled dreams could eat a person's life from the inside out. He had seen it with Marie. And he couldn't stand to see that happen to Naomi Ebersol as well. It was one of the reasons why he prayed that Elam would get back in touch. He wanted to be able to tell his brother that despite whatever dreams had spurred him to walk away from everything that he had... Josias still loved him. Naomi needed that from her family as well.

She heaved a great sigh. "Just for the summer, right?" she asked.

Josias's heart kicked up a notch. "*Jah*, just for the summer."

She stuck her hand to shake his. "Well, then, Josias Schrock, you've got yourself a deal. I'll be your nanny, but not your fiancée."

Chapter Six

She really must be *ab im kopp*. Off in the head. To have agreed to any of this.

But really what choice did she have? She had saved tuition money, but she would also need money to live until she found herself a part-time job there in Philadelphia. As much as she hated to admit it, she needed Josias as much as he needed her.

"That's a first," Evie said, coming out of the post office and watching them seal their deal. "I've never seen an engaged couple shake hands before."

Naomi shot Josias a look she hoped he understood as *you got us into this, now you can get us out of it*, but he seemed not to understand. Or perhaps he was just being a pain.

"We're not engaged," Naomi said, touching her sister's arm as she spoke.

Evie looked from her to Josias. "You're not? But—" She seemed not to know what to say next.

Thankfully Josias stepped forward. "No. We're not."

"But—" Evie shook her head. "Why would Josias say that if it weren't true?"

"I don't know." Naomi crossed her arms, crumbling the

acceptance letter in the crook of her elbow. "Why would you say that?"

He at least had the decency to color at her direct question. And truly she would love an answer, as much as she enjoyed the stain of red seeping all the way to the edge of his hat.

"I was trying to help," he finally managed.

Evie still looked confused, and Naomi couldn't blame her. Josias's off-the-wall declaration was beyond understanding. And yet there was this part of her that wondered why he felt compelled to come to her rescue to begin with. Regardless of the ridiculousness of his solution.

But now was not the time to show gratitude for backhanded rescues. She frowned at him. "Do me a favor and next time you want to do me a favor…don't."

The only good part of Josias's false pronouncement that they were engaged was that Evie had totally forgotten about the letter of acceptance Naomi had received from the art school.

All the way home, Evie could only talk about Josias and if he was all right and speculate on why he had made such an oddball statement. Truthfully, Naomi would like to know herself, but one thing was clear to her now. If he hadn't asserted that they were engaged then she never would have accepted his job offer, but now with school looming ahead she could use the money.

As much as she hated to admit it, Josias was right. Her family knew nothing of her art, nothing of her dreams of being able to draw and paint pieces like those masterpiece paintings she had seen on the calendars in town. She knew they were a poor substitute for the real thing, but those paintings seemed to call to something deep inside her. A longing of belief and yearning that she couldn't explain. And she wanted people to feel that way when they looked at her pictures, like the image before them somehow transformed them, transported them, made them anew.

Pride goeth before the fall. She knew that was the exact reason why drawing and artwork were frowned upon in their community. It wasn't about the individual; it was about the group as a whole and not what the individual could do that no one else could. Not on that level anyway.

And it wasn't like Naomi was planning on staying away forever. She just wanted to know she could do it. Was that so wrong? To want to know that she could be that person? She could produce such beautiful pieces to make the world a more joyous place. There was a part of her that believed that any art she produced simply glorified God. Or maybe it was just the side of her that wanted that recognition telling her things that weren't really true. It was hard to know which was what.

"Has Josias always been this odd?" Evie asked as they drove home.

"I wouldn't say he's odd," Naomi protested.

"Impulsive, then."

Naomi didn't think that was a proper description, either, but she only gave a loose shoulder shrug in objection as she held the reins to the horse pulling their bright yellow buggy. Theirs was the Byler community in the valley as opposed to the Reno or the Nebraska Amish, all holding slightly different beliefs about the church. Yet whereas the Nebraska Amish drove white canvas buggies and the

Reno Amish the shiny black ones, the Byler Amish buggies were bright canary yellow, definitely hard to miss on the roadway.

"He is handsome, though," Evie continued.

"We're not engaged." Naomi said each word succinctly to make sure her sister had no doubts as to the truth.

"I'm just saying." Evie smiled. "But if you're not engaged, why were you shaking hands?"

"I'm going to work for him as a nanny this summer."

"That's exciting."

"Jah." But was it really?

"And then what happens with art school?"

So much for being rescued from her art school dilemma. Now here it was staring her in the face again.

"I don't know," she said, her words only half the truth. She wanted to go, she even *planned* to go, but that didn't mean she would actually *get* to leave. She was splitting hairs, but she had to in order to appease her sister and not tell outright lies.

"So it's not set in stone?" Evie asked.

Naomi hesitated for only a moment before shaking her head.

Evie visibly slumped in relief. "Good. I hate the thought of you going away."

"I just wanted to see if I could get in." That was true. She never fully believed that she would qualify even after all the work she put in to apply—earning her GED and creating a portfolio of work in various mediums.

"I'm glad that's all it is," Evie said. "I need you here for the wedding."

"I'm here." At least for the summer. Would she be after

that? Maybe. And maybe she would have the words to tell her family the whole truth. And maybe, somehow, they would allow her back if only to watch Evie and Freeman get married. But she knew, as much as it broke her heart, that it would not be the case.

"Can you pass me another piece of bread?" Priscilla asked that evening at dinner. Evie and Naomi reached for the basket of bread at the same time, their hands clashing.

Evie started giggling.

So far, Evie had managed to keep Naomi's acceptance into art school a secret, but Naomi knew it was only a matter of time before she let it all slip. For now, Evie was giddy with the idea that Naomi wasn't going to be able to go to art school in the fall because she was somehow magically going to fall in love with Josias as she worked for him this summer. The hardest part for Naomi was that she couldn't protest too much and had to listen to her sister list every positive aspect of the man for the rest of the drive home. Now she was joyfully excited over an outcome that was never going to happen.

All in all, this only delayed the inevitable, but Naomi dreaded trying to explain to her family why art school was so important to her. She didn't see any of them understanding. Not pragmatic Priscilla or blushing Evie. Lizzie was so happy in her job as teacher of the children of their district, Naomi knew she would have a hard time being sympathetic to Naomi's dreams. Perhaps Sarah Ann, the romantic of the family, would understand, but only time would tell. And Naomi wasn't sure how much of that she had. Keeping a secret in this family was sort of like trying to keep the sun from rising in the east.

"Honestly, Evie," Priscilla complained. "Why are you so giggly today?"

Naomi kept her eyes trained on her plate even though she felt Evie's gaze flick to her and away once more.

"No reason." But Evie laughed even as she said the words.

Priscilla pinned Naomi with a hard stare. Though they were as different as twins could possibly be, somehow that shared bond of birth trumped all their differences. "This is on you," Priscilla said.

Naomi inwardly sighed. She hadn't wanted to tackle this now, but no time like the present, *jah*?

"I'm going to work this summer as a nanny for Josias Schrock."

"Dale's father?" Lizzie asked.

She supposed that was one way of describing him.

Evie giggled.

"Okay, so why is Evie giggling like a schoolgirl?" Priscilla asked.

"Because..." Evie started her hazel eyes alight with happiness. "They'll spend the entire summer together—"

"She thinks that if I work for him all summer we will fall in love and get married," Naomi admitted.

"Then she won't—" Evie broke off as Naomi reached under the table and squeezed her hand in warning.

"She won't what?" Lizzie asked.

"I won't be alone." Naomi choked out the words. She hadn't realized it before now, but it had been something she had wondered about. While everyone else around her seemed to be finding love, she still felt like she was adrift, unable to latch on to that future. Or maybe she had known all along that her path would be different.

"Josias Schrock is a good man," her father said.

Evie giggled once more.

"A little old for you, don't you think?" Priscilla pressed.

Naomi shook her head. "Don't worry. Despite our sister's dreams, I have no intentions of falling in love with Josias Schrock."

Once the dishes were done and put away, Naomi managed to escape to the back porch. It was a beautiful night. Crickets were chirping and a light breeze was blowing, and she couldn't help but think of Josias. He hadn't suffered through the evening she had. Because he was only telling his children that he had hired her to be their nanny. He had gotten to tell the truth.

But it's your lie he's trying to protect.

It was hard. Harder than anybody could know. To want something impossible. To have two pieces of your life be at opposite ends of what was expected and what was accepted. And she hated it. Sometimes she asked God why He made her want to draw. Why He put those pictures in her head. Others perhaps would say that it wasn't God who was responsible for the images she saw, for the pictures she wanted to draw, the birds she had to paint, but regardless of its origins those desires were still there. And she had been fighting them for twenty-five years. Sometimes, a woman just got tired of the struggle.

"Naomi?"

She whirled around as her father stepped out onto the

porch. She had forgotten that sometimes he came out here to smoke a pipe and enjoy a bit of quiet. He surely didn't get any of that in their house of chattering females. It had only gotten worse since she and Evie had moved back in. Of course, Evie would be moving out in the fall once she married Freeman Yoder. And Naomi would be moving out to the school, but that was something he didn't know.

"Hi, Dat." She managed a small smile as he came up next to her.

"Need a break from it all?" he asked.

That was something about her *dat* for sure. He was astute. And he did enjoy his quiet. And perhaps she had realized he would come out here tonight. Perhaps she had come out here so she would run into him. It seemed she needed his steady presence to ground her a bit. For a moment there at dinner, she had almost gotten carried away with Evie's spectacular idea of her and Josias falling in love and getting married. She never thought about herself and marriage. Never really imagined getting married. While all her other friends at school were playing house and pretending what they would do when they did get married, she would rather play baseball with the boys.

She nodded as he stepped closer. She was immediately soothed by the warmth of his presence. The familiarity of him.

"Why do I feel like you want to tell me something?" It was a dangerous question. Probably one that she shouldn't have asked, but it was free in the night air before she could stop herself.

"You could do worse than Josias Schrock."

"I'm just going to work for him," she stated. "And only for the summer."

"I know." Her father nodded. "I know. But sometimes when people get close, even when they are only working together, things can happen. Feelings change.

"I suppose," she murmured. "But that's not my goal."

Her *dat* shook his head and sighed. "You are so much like your mother, you know."

She had heard this her entire life, how much she favored her mother, the only difference being the blue light in her eyes that her mother didn't have. According to everyone she knew, her mother's eyes were as green as bottle glass. "So I've been told."

"No." Her father shook his head. "Not just in looks. You are so much like her in here." He tapped calloused fingers against his chest where his heart beat. "She was… restless, too."

She opened her mouth to debunk the idea that she was restless but closed it against that lie to herself. "I didn't know."

"*Jah*," her father said quietly. "Sometimes I would come out here and find her just looking off at the sky."

Naomi wasn't sure how to respond to that, so she waited for her father to continue.

"I guess what I'm trying to say is sometimes our goals change, and you could do worse than Josias Schrock."

"You've already said that."

He chuckled at himself. "The problem with being restless," he started, "is that you have to find someone worthy of settling down for."

Naomi let those words whirl around her until they made

a semblance of sense. "Are you saying that if Mamm hadn't married you then she would've left Millers Creek?"

He shrugged there in the dim light of the porch. "I'm just saying I'm lucky that she loved me more than she wanted to see what was out there."

"How did you talk me into this?"

Josias bit back a chuckle. He figured that he had laughed more around Naomi Ebersol than he had in all the months since Marie had passed.

Don't get used to it.

"Hey," he said. "I was just trying to help you out. You're welcome to go back and tell your family the truth."

He could almost see her mulling over the repercussions of doing just that.

"Of course, this way you'll at least have the money from your summer job."

"Summer job," she muttered. "I'm not twelve."

No, she was not. "It's up to you." He said the words even as he secretly prayed that she would not turn him down. Yes, he needed a nanny in the worst sort of way. But there were more women in the valley than just Naomi Ebersol. He could find someone—Amish, English or even Mennonite—to help him take care of his boys this summer. But there was something about Naomi Ebersol that made him want to spend more time with her. Chalk it up to his uncanny ability to pick the wrong woman. Just like Marie. They were right for each other in every way but her restlessness. He could see that same yearning in Naomi's eyes.

She was taking too long to answer.

"You're leaving in the fall, right?"

He couldn't help but notice she hesitated before answering. Not a great deal, just a small little pause. *"Jah."*

"That is perfect."

She crossed her arms, the strings of her prayer *kapp* brushing over her shoulders as she tilted her head to one side. "Why do you only need me for the summer? You only have one boy in school, so it's not like you haven't been doing this for months."

Now that was a question he didn't want to answer. He opted for the easy way out. "Mamm and Esther were helping, but now that Helen is back and gone again and Mamm with her…" Maybe it wasn't the easy way out.

"You think they're going to be gone for the summer. Then when they come back, you'll have help again."

"Exactly." He breathed a small sigh of relief that he wouldn't have to explain any more than that. The truth had been hard enough on his family as it was.

"It's odd," Naomi continued. "Helen breaks up with Freeman, runs off to Lancaster, then comes back and now runs off to New Wilmington."

She wasn't telling him anything he didn't already know. It did look odd to the outsider, but he knew that it wouldn't be long before they would have to tell the truth. Depending on what decision his parents and Helen came to about the baby.

Then the thought occurred to him. He hadn't done the math before, but Helen wouldn't have this baby until about Christmastime, which would mean she wouldn't be back at the end of summer. Not with a swollen belly and no husband. He couldn't imagine his *mamm* coming back without Helen.

"What is it?" Naomi demanded.

Josias shook his head.

"What? Did you change your mind?"

"No," he said quickly. "I didn't change my mind about anything." Except what he was going to do at the end of summer when Naomi left for art school. He supposed he had a little time to find someone else to take her place.

"Something is going on," she said, eyeing him shrewdly.

"Why do you say that?" Perhaps he shouldn't have asked that.

"Helen's acting all goofy. Now you need a nanny, your *mamm*'s run off with Helen to who knows where, and Freeman is getting married to Evie…"

"Has anyone ever told you that you have a suspicious mind?"

"It comes with the territory."

"I'm sorry? What?"

"Being Amish. We're not really suspicious, but what else do we have to do but worry about each other and pray for each other? The only way to do that is to know what's going on with each other."

He couldn't argue with that. Just the mention of the word *prayer* had him contemplating telling her all right then and there. But he couldn't. He might know her secrets—that Naomi was leaving for the English world in a few months to pursue her passion for art—but the secret he was keeping was not his to tell.

Chapter Seven

"You know farm work doesn't end."

Naomi ignored the grumble in Josias's voice. It was barely discernible over the racket his boys were making in the back seat. But they weren't fighting or arguing or otherwise annoying one another. They were simply excited to be going to the last day of school picnic.

Even though Dale was the only one who was in school, the family all came out on the last day to celebrate another school year gone past. It'd been years since Naomi had gone to one, and probably Josias, too. He had tried everything to get out of attending this morning, but she had told him Dale was his child and he was going. Oddly enough, it felt almost like being a wife lecturing him on his fatherly duties. But now that they were almost to the schoolhouse, she was having her own reservations.

Maybe it wasn't a good idea for them to all attend together. Maybe it would've been better if she had insisted Josias come without her. But he hadn't wanted to attend alone, stating that he had hired a nanny to help him handle his children for the summer and he couldn't very well do that all by himself. Faced with his convoluted logic, Naomi had given up and gathered the boys to get ready to go to the picnic. Plus, with those words she understood his reluctance to take care of them by himself, maybe even further understood why he had meddled in her life. He was afraid of messing up as a single father. And perhaps that also explained why he was so reluctant to attend the picnic.

It was true that most Amish families were role oriented. When one of those roles was no longer filled, it left a hole and a big learning curve for the remaining partner. He would be fine, given time. And it seemed she would be his buffer, support system and helper until then.

"It'll be fun," Naomi said. But she wasn't sure if she was trying to convince him or herself. It *was* going to be fun. Well, she hoped it would be anyway.

They turned into the lane that led to the one-room schoolhouse, and Naomi could see all the yellow buggies parked off to one side. The adjacent pasture was already filled with carriage horses chomping on the grass and otherwise waiting for their owners to finish celebrating this final day of school. Her sister Lizzie was standing on the porch next to Sarah Ann, the youngest Ebersol daughter, as they pulled in and parked. In no time at all, the horse was released into the pasture, and the boys were running across the field to join the picnic.

Naomi turned to Josias. "I'll go put the lunches on the porch," she said, gesturing with one hand in that general direction.

"You do that," he said.

Naomi spun on her heel and walked as quickly as she could without running to where her sisters waited. Why was everything suddenly so awkward? Because she could see her sisters dreaming possibilities as they watched them approach. She was practically breathless when she got to the schoolhouse porch.

"It's so strange to see you with Josias," Sarah Ann said, that dreamy quality in her voice. As far as Sarah Ann was concerned, there was nothing better than a good romance.

"*Jah*," Naomi said, realizing that her response didn't match her sister's statement. "Anyway," she continued, "here are our lunches." She held the cooler full of sandwiches and waters up as if to show them proof.

"Wouldn't it be something if Evie is right and the two of you end up married?"

"That's not going to happen. I am merely working for him." Naomi hoped her words penetrated Sarah Ann's fantasy world. Sometimes when she got a hold of something it was hard to convince her to let it go.

"Why does he need a nanny again?" Lizzie asked.

"His *mamm* and Helen have been helping him since Marie died, and now they are off in New Wilmington."

Sarah Ann nodded. "Do you suppose that Helen left because of Freeman and Evie?"

Lizzie shook her head. "I think something else is going on there."

So did Naomi, and she was also glad that the subject had slipped from her and Josias.

"Have you talked to Josias about it?" Sarah Ann asked.

"Why would I talk to him about it?" Naomi asked.

"Because you might get married soon," Lizzie said, her voice once again rising above Naomi's comfort level.

"We are not getting married, and it'll do no good to pretend like we are." Naomi placed one finger over her lips as if to emphasize her command.

Sarah Ann nodded and made a mime like she was locking her lips closed. If only...

Truly Sarah Ann was as bad as Evie. Maybe even worse. Evie had only recently been gung ho for everyone to be in love, but Sarah Ann had always been a little boy crazy.

Naomi recognized that her words were unkind, and she was glad they were only expressed in her mind. She wouldn't want her sister to know what she was thinking. And perhaps Sarah Ann wasn't really boy crazy and Naomi was just the opposite. What was the opposite of boy crazy? She had no idea.

"He's a smart one to hire you," Lizzie said. "You'll have that house whipped into shape in no time."

"What makes you think it's not in shape?" Naomi asked, even as the image of Josias's kitchen with dishes piled on every available surface passed through her mind. It was going to take a full day to just get the kitchen in order.

"He wouldn't have hired you to help him if he didn't need help," Lizzie matter-of-factly stated.

Good point.

"Unless it's just for the wedding," Sarah Ann said in a singsong voice.

Naomi was just about to correct her when a small gasp came from the end of the porch. Naomi whirled around to see Imogene Peight, the biggest gossip in all of Millers Creek, standing there, brown-bag picnic lunches in one hand and mouth hanging open.

Great. Just great, Naomi thought. *Let the rumors begin.*

"I can't believe, that of all people to have overheard something like that, that it had to be Imogene Peight."

Naomi crossed her arms and huffed. "Well, believe it," she said. "It seems to be just my luck these days."

It was almost four o'clock in the afternoon, and she was exhausted. Taking care of her sister's three sweet little girls was much different than running after five rowdy boys. Much, much different. Now she knew exactly why Josias wanted a nanny. Boys were work.

"*Your* luck?" He shook his head. "So, I suppose the entire community will know by…"

"Tomorrow lunch at the latest."

She had meant that as a joke, but he nodded sagely. "*Jah*. We may have that long."

"I'm sorry," she said. "Really, really sorry. I tried to explain to Imogene that Sarah Ann was just imagining things, but I know she wasn't hearing me."

He nodded, then swallowed hard. "I understand. I just don't want that rumor getting back to the boys."

"Of course not," she said, remorse filling her even though this was a problem of his own making. If he hadn't said at the post office that the two of them were engaged then Evie would have never said anything in front of Sarah Ann, and in turn, she wouldn't have spilled the beans— *fake* beans, as it were—to Imogene. But now was not the time to point that out to him. "School's out, and when are they going to have an opportunity to listen to adults talk?"

"Sunday at church," he said.

"And how many times when you were a kid did you stop to listen to adults other than whoever was preaching when you were at church? Even at mealtime?"

"Good point. But I'm still worried."

She could see that by the frown puckered between his

dark eyebrows. This was more of the look she had known him to have these last few months. Ever since his wife died. But it seemed like recently he had been smiling and laughing. She hated that now he was back to a frown.

"Play it by ear, I suppose," she said. "If someone says something, one of the boys will come to us, and we'll tell them the truth."

"And if they don't believe us?"

She was afraid he was going to ask that. "I don't know. Perhaps you shouldn't have told my family that we were engaged to begin with."

He gave a small, almost hesitant nod. "I suppose you're right about that."

Suddenly, Naomi was flooded with even more remorse. She shouldn't have snapped at him. Now she wanted to reach up and smooth that frown off his forehead. Instead, she shoved her hand under the band of her apron and nodded along with him. "Chances are the boys won't hear anything at church because they're not going to be still long enough to hear any adults talk about things that they aren't interested in."

"I hope you're right."

"Me, too," she said. "So, I guess I'll see you in the morning?"

"You're leaving?"

She almost winced at the panic she heard in his voice. "*Jah*. It's almost four o'clock."

"Exactly," he said. "What about dinner? I've got cows to milk, and the boys haven't had their baths and—" He stopped. "You know, it's fine."

But she could tell from his tone it was anything but fine.

"If I leave now, what will you have for supper?"

"Sandwiches. I think I got some soup left in there still. The kind from a can," he clarified. "I don't do homemade soup. Like, I can't make it or anything."

Each word was like a little stab to her heart. She couldn't leave. This was exactly what he hired her to do…but it had been a long day already.

"Even with as much time as I spend with Mattie and her girls, I don't think I realized just how much parenting is a full-time job."

A small smile played at the corners of his lips. "Don't I know it. I found out the hard way."

That he did. She supposed he had been eased into it a little bit. Marie had been sick before she died, some mysterious ailment that no one could exactly name. Some said it was a broken heart. Not two months before, she had buried a baby girl born too soon and unable to survive.

Naomi pushed the thought away before tears could sting her eyes. She had no idea what she would've done in that situation. Didn't even want to think about it. Even if she didn't plan on having a husband and children of her own, she couldn't imagine burying one or the other. She had seen what it did to her sisters, Priscilla and Mattie both. And frankly, she couldn't tell if all the pain was worth it.

She wondered how Josias felt about it but thought better than to ask.

"I'll stay."

"You don't have to—you've already been here well over a workday."

"And if I don't stay, what are you going to do?"

He shrugged. "Not sure. But I'll figure something out."

"That doesn't seem quite fair," she said. "You're paying me to be your nanny and I'm not here when you need a person the most?"

"Fine," he said. "I guess I shouldn't argue with you."

She grinned at him. "You got that right."

Josias headed out to the barn, and Naomi made her way back into the house. The boys were all sitting around the dining room table playing with a puzzle. It looked like it had been sitting there for quite some time, and the boys had been working on it in the way only young boys can. Some pieces were forced together, the colors not matching, some were upside down with the back of the puzzle piece showing instead of the picture on the front, but they were quiet and seemed to be having a good time.

Thankfully it only took a half hour to get the main counter clean enough she could think about cooking.

"Let's see what we can find for dinner," she said. "Anyone want to help?" Four little hands shot into the air. Only Tommy didn't realize what was going on at first but raised his to match his brothers, unwilling to be left out.

Naomi bit back her smile. Children were always so enthusiastic.

She wasn't sure what she would find in the kitchen to cook, and she wasn't sure how helpful her little helpers would be, but she was here to do a job, and she was going to do it.

"What's your favorite food?" Naomi asked as she peered into the refrigerator.

"Macaroni and cheese."

"Hamburgers with cheese."

"French fries. No wait, spaghetti. No wait, cheeseburgers."

"You already said that."

"No, you said hamburgers with cheese."

"That's the same thing." The last voice was a different addition, and she recognized it as Dale's.

"No arguing," she said without turning around. The refrigerator was stocked fairly well considering the man was a widower with small children. He must've recently gone to the store. There were packages of meat stacked neatly, a large block of cheese, a gallon and a half of milk and a big container of orange juice. She supposed the pantry was equally stocked. At least she hoped it was.

She grabbed a couple of pounds of ground beef out of the refrigerator and closed the door. Then she turned around to face the tribe. "How about cheeseburger macaroni?"

The boys looked at her, confused.

"What's that?" Harley asked. At least she thought it was Harley. Then she remembered. He was the one who looked just like Josias. Same gray-blue eyes, same dark brown hair. Who knew, by the end of the summer she might even get all of their names correct.

"You've never had cheeseburger macaroni?" It was a house favorite at the Ebersols'.

All five boys shook their heads. They were all out of sync and it almost made her dizzy to watch.

"Well, then, it's macaroni and cheese plus hamburger plus vegetables—"

"Ew."

"Who said that?" she asked.

All fingers pointed toward Eli.

His cheeks turned pink, but he grinned at her. Both of his front teeth were missing. Considering the fact that he was only five, she wondered if he had lost them early or if he had knocked them out doing some reckless feat that only a boy would attempt.

"So, you don't like vegetables?"

He shook his head, still grinning.

"That's why you put them in with the cheese. Vegetables with cheese on them are always best."

Dale's mouth fell open. "You'll give us vegetables with cheese?"

"Don't you think they'll taste better?"

He nodded vigorously.

"Well, the whole point is to eat them, right?"

All the boys nodded.

"Well, then, you've got to make them taste good. Now, who's with me?"

The boys all raised their hands once again and jumped into action, fetching macaroni from the pantry along with a can of English peas and baby carrots. It wasn't her favorite. She really liked to add a little bit of corn to it as well, but it would do for tonight. She quickly located the large iron skillet and began frying up the ground beef. She chopped the onion and peppers, added some garlic, then set the macaroni on to boil.

Before long Josias came in, looking around at the scene before him. Naomi wondered what it looked like. She had all the boys at the table working on something or another for their supper. She was afraid by the time Eli was done there wouldn't be anything but pulp and seeds left of the tomato he was chopping, but she had given him a butter knife to do his work. Couldn't have them cutting their fingers off in the name of helping.

"Something smells good," he said. Again, he was smiling, and Naomi began to wonder if she imagined all those frowns before.

The boys jumped up from the table, all bouncing around him and telling him what was for supper.

"And we're going to have vegetables with cheese on them," Eli said.

Naomi felt her cheeks redden as Josias pinned her with a stare. "I hope that's okay?" It should've been a statement, but it came out more like a question. She supposed she should've asked about any dietary requirements they might have, but it was too late to consider them for tonight's dinner.

"If you can get him to eat vegetables, you can slather on all the cheese you want." He smiled. "I just wish I'd thought of it myself."

Her cheeks flamed. She waved a hand in front of her face. "Whew. The stove is really heating things up in here." That was her excuse, and she was sticking to it.

She wondered if perhaps he realized that he had made her uncomfortable because he immediately shooed his kids back to the table and told them he was going to wash up.

He disappeared up the steps, and Naomi was once again left alone with five chattering boys and a huge pan of cheeseburger macaroni. They seemed to enjoy helping her get everything together, sliding it into the oven and setting the timer so they would know when to pull it out again. Then she got them all working setting places at the table for everyone to eat.

Perhaps Josias was waiting until the food was ready before coming back down the stairs or maybe he had impeccable timing. Either way, she was just pulling the pan from the oven and placing it in the middle of the table on the hot pads Harley had laid there for just that purpose when Josias reentered the kitchen. His eyes widened at the scene in front of him.

"What?" Naomi asked.

"Nothing." But he smiled when he said it.

"There's something going on," she said, propping her hands on her hips.

He shook his head. "It's just been a long time since I came down and dinner was ready, and the table was set, and the boys were...behaving."

Naomi looked around the kitchen just to make sure there was nothing that she had forgotten. She made the boys wash their hands before helping with supper and after, and everyone was sitting, waiting mostly patiently to eat vegetables with cheese on them.

"Well," she said. "Go ahead and sit down."

He made his way to the head of the table and stopped once again, assessing plates, napkins, forks, chairs, boys and the opposite end of the table that was bare.

"Aren't you going to eat?"

"I thought I would grab something when I got home."

"You're leaving?" The question came from both Josias and Dale.

The younger boys all begin to cry *no*. And *don't go*. Even as she dried her hands on a dish towel.

"It's time for you guys to have your evening together."

"I thought that you'd at least stay and eat," Josias said quietly. Something in his tone gave her pause.

"I—I..." She didn't have the words. She thought she

would go home. Her work was done. It would begin again tomorrow morning. She would get the kids up, and they would begin their new summer routine, whatever that might be. She had a feeling it was going to include feeding chickens, chasing cats and working on the garden plot she had seen off to one side. It was getting late in the season to start a house garden, but she couldn't imagine a house without one. "You want me to stay and eat with you?"

"Jah." The one word resounded. Josias gave her a strange look, somewhere between a frown and a tender smile. She couldn't figure out which was the most prominent. "Of course, we want you to stay and eat with us." And yet, she had the feeling those words were more for his children's benefit than hers. That was what she chose to believe anyway.

She swallowed hard. "My family is expecting me home. I wouldn't want to worry them." And it was the truth. Her family was expecting her, and there was no way she could let them know she would be late. "Just leave the supper dishes in the sink. I can take care of them in the morning."

"It's Saturday tomorrow."

She hadn't thought about that. Though she couldn't say why, she felt a strong urge to get out of there. She couldn't pinpoint the exact reason, but it was time for her to go. But then how could she if the supper dishes were something he expected of her every night as part of her duties? He had hired her to watch his sons and clean.

"Just go," he told her.

"You're leaving?" Ivan seemed to only then understand that she wasn't staying with them permanently. He jumped up from his chair and raced to her side, hugging her around the waist.

The rest of the boys jumped up to hug her as well.

All but Tommy, who was struggling to figure out how to release himself from his high chair. May the good Lord help them when he finally did. They had a tough time now just trying to keep him contained.

"I'll miss you," Ivan said. "When will you come back? You will come back, *jah*?"

She almost broke down at the earnest look on his face. One day his *mamm* had disappeared. Not literally, but she had been there and then she was gone. She could understand that he was reluctant to see another mother figure leave.

Maybe this nanny idea wasn't such a good one. She wouldn't want the children to get ideas that weren't going to happen. Like her becoming a permanent fixture in their household. She was only doing this to get money for school. Come fall she was out of here. Out of Millers Creek, out of the valley.

"Of course. I'll be back Monday morning," she promised, looking up just in time to catch their father's gaze.

Josias frowned at her. But she didn't take the time to ask him what the problem was. Their food was getting cold, and she needed to be getting home.

Josias was more than reluctant to see her go. And it had nothing to do with the fact that his children were begging her to stay and demanding to know when she was coming back. Nor did it have anything to do with giving five boys a bath. Dale could pretty much take care of himself, and then he put them in the tub two at a time, and in no time at all, he had five squeaky-clean boys. It was just that he missed her. Maybe not Naomi herself but having that companion. He didn't think he wanted to get married again, and yet he found himself yearning for that connection, the togetherness that a woman brought.

When it was just his *mamm* and his sister coming over to help, he felt that it was the adult companionship, the full circle, but now that he had Naomi here, he realized it was something more. If only he wasn't so terrible at trying to find a wife. Maybe he should go to one of those matchmakers. Maybe he should if he truly wanted to get married again.

He pushed the thought away and went up the stairs behind his little family. They all piled up on the bed that Dale and Ivan shared so that he could read them a story. As usual, Tommy fell asleep on the end of the bed, and, as usual, he woke up as Josias tried to put him in his crib.

Josias spent the next fifteen minutes patting the boy on the back and reassuring him that the world was still a good place. Finally, when Tommy drifted off to sleep, Josias made his way into the other two bedrooms and tucked in his other sons, kissing them on their foreheads and wishing them a good night. He asked if they said their prayers, even as he was still wishing that Naomi was there.

It was a thought that didn't bear further examination. Because Naomi was never going to be there. And because he wasn't getting married again. This was his family now. He might as well get used to it.

He made his way downstairs and ran the sink full of water. He was bone weary. Even having Naomi there during the day to watch over the boys and cook and clean, he was still tired. He supposed he might always be. Five boys and a farm were a lot for a single father. Even with a full-time nanny.

Maybe that was because a wife was more than full time. Having a wife was a 24-7 endeavor, but not one he was willing to engage in again.

He finished up the kitchen, then eased down into his favorite chair, watching the flame of the kerosene lamp dance on the table next to him. He had other means of lighting his house, but he did enjoy the kerosene lantern. Maybe because Marie had picked it out. Or maybe because it was just old-fashioned enough to remind him why they did some of the things they did. Why they stayed married and didn't divorce. Why they wore conservative clothing, drove horses and buggies, and turned their back on the world in general.

Most who were widowed married again, usually within the year of mourning. There were families to care for, after all, and most Amish families were large. Even larger than his own.

He whispered a small prayer under his breath. He wouldn't be in this situation had it not been for tragedies and blessings and those mixed with both. But here he sat listening to the house creak, wondering if his decisions were correct and still thinking about Naomi Ebersol.

Maybe he should go see a matchmaker, see if he could figure out a better wife for himself. Marie had wanted other things, but she had not been bold enough to go after them. She only dreamed about what could have been. Then once she had the one thing that he thought would settle her down and make her content—a daughter—they had lost her. After that, he had lost Marie. Now both were buried in the cemetery just down the road, and he was forever tethered to Millers Creek.

A small part of him envied Naomi and her freedom to leave. She was going off to art school, going to find that different thing that she and Marie had both dreamt of. And she would leave him behind.

Chapter Eight

"Where to now?" Lizzie asked.

Naomi bit back the reply that sprang immediately to her lips. "Home, then to Josias's." But that wasn't right. It was Saturday, and she wasn't going to work today. She had made enough food last night that the Schrocks would have leftovers for the weekend, then Monday she would be back to cook again. Josias had assured her that the arrangement would work, and that Esther would come during his milking times on Saturday and Sunday to help watch Tommy.

But still Naomi worried. She had learned firsthand those boys were a handful. They were fine and energetic and rowdy and inquisitive, and they never stopped. Or maybe it was just that there were five of them. If one stopped, another one picked up where he had left off. And she wondered how Josias was doing.

"What is wrong with you?" Lizzie asked, elbowing her in the side gently, playfully, but enough to jar her out of her thoughts.

"Nothing, I was just…thinking."

"About what?" Sarah Ann joined the conversation. "Josias?"

"As a matter of fact…"

Lizzie laughed. "You have got it so bad."

"No—" Naomi cut off her own denial. "I just hate leaving him on the weekends. Those boys." She smiled as she said it. "They're a handful, and he's got cows to milk and—" She broke off. "Is that Esther Schrock?"

The girls turned to see Esther come out of the fabric store, a package in one hand.

"Looks like her to me," Lizzie quipped. "Now, don't you think it's time to get ice cream?"

"I absolutely remember ice cream being brought up," Sarah Ann said.

Naomi shook her head. "Esther is supposed to be helping Josias today."

"All day?" Sarah Ann asked. "I mean, maybe she went this morning when he was milking."

But Naomi had seen how much needed to be done around the farm, and with five boys under foot... Well, if they were a couple of years older it would be entirely different, but they weren't. Little Tommy was barely two years old.

She broke away from her sisters and started across the road.

"Where are you going?" Lizzie called after her.

"I'll be right back," Naomi threw over one shoulder.

She raced to catch up with Esther.

"Esther! Hey!" She practically ran across the parking lot to reach her before she hopped in her buggy. "I thought you were at Josias's today."

Esther turned in surprise. "Hi, Naomi. What was that?"

Naomi sucked in a big gulp of air to try to catch her breath. "I thought you were going to Josias's house today to help him with the boys."

A small frown creased her brow. "I told him I have to help Dat today."

"So, no one's there with Josias?"

Esther's frown deepened. "I'm sure he's okay. I mean, he didn't say he needed any help."

Naomi shook her head, more to get her thoughts in order than to negate anything that Esther was telling her. "You think he's fine?"

Esther didn't immediately answer. "I heard the two of you are engaged."

Naomi closed her eyes and wished for the rumor to go away, but she knew when she opened them once more, it would still be there, hanging over her like a big black cloud. Just how many people would find out? That was the question.

"Have you talked to Josias about it?" She wouldn't want to step on anything that he had already told his sister. And she didn't think that he would tell her about Naomi going to art school. But if it came down to betraying Naomi or taking the fall himself, she had a feeling this whole ruse would be overcome tomorrow afternoon.

"Just that things happened sort of fast between the two of you," Esther said.

Huh? "Well... I mean... I—" Naomi really didn't know what to say. It wasn't true, but she had a feeling that Esther already had her mind made up. If Imogene Peight said it, it had to be real.

"He's a good man, my brother," Esther continued. "I don't want to see him get his heart broken."

Naomi shook her head. "I would never do anything to hurt your brother." That was the honest truth. She had no reason, no call, to break Josias's heart. This whole engagement ruse was his idea. But of course, Esther knew none of that.

"Marie…" Esther began. But she broke off without finishing the thought. "His heart is fragile," she started once more. "I see how he looks at you."

When had that happened? "I don't know what that means."

"Like he wished things could be different. And if you're getting married and he wants things to be different…"

Naomi wasn't sure how to respond. She wanted to flat-out tell Esther that she was seeing things, but Naomi didn't know that for certain. All she knew was that he had told her that he never wanted to get married again and he needed a nanny while he waited for his *mamm* to come back from New Wilmington. There were probably a lot of things he wished could be different that had nothing to do with her.

"Esther," Naomi said, "I promise you I would never do anything to hurt Josias."

Sunday after church and Josias could feel everyone watching him. It felt that way at least. Everywhere he went, it seemed like people were smiling more, nodding more, in general seeming to act as if they were in on a secret. For the first time he truly regretted his chivalrous act of trying to save Naomi from herself. Or her family. It depended on how a person looked at it.

"It seems you're the talk of the town," his brother Levi said, raising his little Styrofoam cup of water in salute.

"That's really funny." Josias took up a position next to him against the long wooden fence that made up one side of the corral. He was aware of the picture they made, near twin-like in appearance, with their similar height and dark brown hair. But where Josias had inherited their mother's gray-blue eyes, Levi boasted the amber brown of their father. "It's fake." He didn't know why he told his brother that again. He had told his brother and his father the truth when Esther came home yesterday with the news that she had found out about the engagement. She was hurt that Josias hadn't told her himself. And despite the fact that he told her it wasn't the truth, that he and Naomi were never engaged, it seemed that Esther didn't believe him. Too many people were spreading the rumor, and too many couples in the past had done everything in their power to keep their engagements a secret. It was an Amish custom followed by many. So no matter how much he and Naomi protested, those around them thought they were just being secretive.

"That's what you keep saying," Levi said, his gaze trained on the whole of the church district as everyone milled around and prepared to eat their after-church meal. Normally this was a fun time for Josias. His work during the week kept him away from his family, and so this was a good time to reconnect. He just didn't want to reconnect over an engagement that never happened.

"She's my nanny," he said. "Just until Mamm comes back. End of the summer at the latest."

Levi turned to him with a frown. "Mamm is not coming back by the end of the summer."

That was exactly what Josias had been afraid of. "A guy can hope."

"Hope all you want. It's not going to change anything. I don't see her coming back until Christmas. If then."

Josias shook his head. "She can't stay gone that long."

"She'll stay as long as she needs to get everything settled."

And such was the problem with trying to discuss the delicate matter of Helen's baby. Neither one wanted to say the words out loud and surely would not do it at a church service, where anyone could overhear.

"But Christmas?"

"What about Christmas?"

Both men turned as their father sauntered up.

Even at sixty, Elmer Schrock cut an impressive figure. He was as tall and broad as both his sons, though his once dark brown hair was now completely gray. He wore his marriage beard long and untrimmed as was the tradition of the older generation.

Josias found so much hair to be itchy and trimmed his on occasion, and since Levi had never been married, he boasted no beard at all. Josias wondered whether, if his brother turned forty without being married, he would grow a beard like some of the confirmed bachelors in their community had done before him.

"My brother here thinks Mamm will be back before Christmas," Levi said wryly.

Elmer stopped and stroked his beard, his thoughtful gesture. Josias recognized it immediately. "Well, now, that's hard to say, but I don't see it happening."

Levi glanced around as if making sure no one was close enough to overhear. "I figure she'll go see Hannah."

It was something that Josias had wondered about himself. Could Helen have a baby and then just bring it back to their community? He knew when she returned she would be required to ask for forgiveness, but the child would most likely remain somewhere else. Josias had wondered if that somewhere else might be with their childless sister, Hannah.

Hannah was the oldest of all the Schrock children and had married Reuben Zook nearly a decade before. Still, the couple remained a family of two. It seemed only logical that they would care for Helen's out-of-wedlock child. Otherwise, Josias wasn't sure what would become of Helen. But he couldn't imagine giving up one of his own children, even to one of his siblings. His heart went out to Helen. *Jah*, she had made mistakes. Big mistakes. Mistakes and sins that required a great deal of prayer and forgiveness, but he wouldn't wish giving up a child on anyone. And definitely not a sister he dearly loved.

"If she's not coming back for a while, then I'll just have to figure something else out," Josias said. He had a nanny for a couple of months. As far as he was concerned, that gave him a couple of months to find a better solution to his problem.

"You know, you could always just get remarried," his father said.

It wasn't that Josias had to listen to the argument often, but he knew his parents had been thinking about it, most probably talking about it once everyone else had gone to bed. It simply seemed to be the way. When he sat down and thought about it himself—or overthought about it—it did seem the most logical course of action. Amish communities were about community. About family. About togetherness. And in his case, that togetherness was a little bit fractured since a *mamm* and wife was missing from the picture. *Jah*, he could fill the hole for a while and call that solution a nanny, but they all knew the best and most permanent solution would be to find a new wife. It wasn't a thought he relished. Because unless he found another widow to marry, a woman with children of her own already, whoever he married would most likely want to have more babies. He knew that was God's plan. But after burying his baby Annabelle, Josias just wasn't sure he had the heart for it. He buried a part of himself with that tiny little body, a part he knew he would never get back. It had been as hard on him as it had been on Marie, the only difference was he managed to dig his way out of that black fog of grief while Marie had succumbed.

"I know, I know," Josias murmured. Hoping that answer would at least stay any more arguments in favor of him remarrying. They were sure to come in the future, and he could deal with that. But today he was not in the mood.

"You know what would save a lot of time and effort," Levi said, giving him a strange look.

"What is that?" Josias asked. Then he had a feeling he might regret that decision.

"You could marry your fake fiancée."

Marry my fake fiancée. Josias chased that thought around inside his brain as he set the table for supper that night. It was a Sunday, and as usual he had left the service a little bit early to come home and milk his cows. Now he was setting the table for their simple dinner of cold cuts, cheese and crackers.

Yet he couldn't help but wonder what his fake fiancée was doing tonight. As she had promised, there had been enough food left in the refrigerator, and all had been organized where he could see the meal at the ready. Like tonight. She had placed slices of meat and cheese on a tray and stuck a little piece of paper on top of it that said *Serve with crackers. Sunday.* So that was just what he was doing.

"Can we have some applesauce, too?" Dale asked.

The kid could live on applesauce alone, Josias was certain. He supposed it was a good thing they had an apple tree in the backyard, otherwise they might go broke supplying him with apples.

"Of course." Josias turned back to the refrigerator to fetch the jar of pulverized fruit. Then he remembered. All the many jars that Marie used to get out on Sunday evenings. Olives, pickles, chowchow, and of course, applesauce. He started pulling jars out and grabbing spoons so the children could help themselves to a little something tangy on the side. Then he speared a pickle for Tommy and set it on his high chair tray.

See? He could do this. For a while anyway. Then what? He didn't want to get remarried. Were there really any other choices?

"Is there going to be a wedding?" Dale asked.

Josias almost got a crick in his neck as he swung his head around quickly to look at his son. "What?" Surely he hadn't heard that correctly.

"I asked, is there going to be a wedding?"

He had to field this one very carefully. "What makes you ask that?" That was probably the best place to start.

"Everyone keeps talking about people getting married. When you get married you have to have a wedding, right?"

Josias swallowed hard and nodded. "That's right."

"So, is there going to be a wedding?"

If his son had heard something about him and Naomi getting married, surely he would've said that outright. Still Josias had to proceed with caution. "Who is getting married? Did you hear their names?"

He waited breathlessly for his son to continue. It was one thing to pull the wool over their families' eyes and say that they were getting married and another for his children to believe that to be the truth. The ruse might be ending before it even got good and started. "Freeman Yoder and Evie Ebersol," Dale said.

"I like Evie," Ivan said, swinging his legs as he chomped on a cracker.

"I like Naomi," Harley said.

Dale turned and frowned at his brother. "Freeman isn't gonna marry Naomi. He's marrying Evie."

"Who is marrying Naomi?"

"I don't think—" Josias started but couldn't finish. He tried again. "Yes, Dale, Freeman and Evie are getting married sometime soon. Just like Mattie and Samuel got married."

"I like Samuel," Eli said, still bouncing his legs and eating his crackers. Tiny crumbs flew from his mouth as he spoke.

"I like Samuel, too," Josias said. "Don't talk with your mouth full."

"*Jah*, Dat," Eli said, still spewing more crackers.

Josias mentally shook his head. Boys would be boys, he presumed.

"Why do people get married?" Ivan asked.

Josias had never missed Marie more than he did in that

moment. "To make families." It was a quick answer, but he was satisfied with it. It made perfect sense that people got married so there could be families.

"But in our family," Dale started, that frown creasing his forehead as he spoke, "there's no wife. Not since Mamm..."

"Sometimes," Josias said, choosing each word carefully. "Sometimes a family loses a *mamm* or *dat*, but they still go on being a family. That never stops."

Dale seemed to think about it for a moment. Then he turned to look at Ivan to gauge what his brother thought about the matter. But Ivan was too busy wrapping his olives in little strips of ham to give the conversation much more attention.

"So, it's okay then," Dale asked. "It's okay that we don't have a *mamm* anymore?"

No, it wasn't okay. It wasn't okay that Marie had died. It wasn't okay that the boys lost their baby sister. It wasn't okay that Josias lost his wife. But it was just the way it was. Still, he knew what Dale was asking.

"Did someone say something?" Josias asked.

"Rose, Elise and Christie were talking about it on the last day of school. I overheard them. But I don't think they knew I was there."

Rose, Elise and Christie were the daughters of Imogene Peight, the biggest gossip in the county. And seeing as how Imogene was the one responsible for spreading the rumors about Josias and Naomi, he could only hope that the daughters hadn't heard that one yet.

"And what were they saying?" He wasn't sure he wanted to know.

"Just that Naomi went with us to the picnic because we didn't have a *mamm* anymore."

"That's true actually," Josias said. "She's coming to help us for the summer because we don't have a *mamm* anymore, and Mammi and Helen are away on a trip."

"What about Esther?" Ivan asked. "She was helping. Can she be our *mamm*?"

"I like Esther," Eli said.

"You like everybody," Dale countered.

"What's wrong with that?" Eli shot back.

Ivan was still staring at Josias, waiting for an answer.

"Esther can't be your *mamm* because she's your aunt. My sister."

"What about Naomi then?" Ivan demanded. "She's not your sister, and she went with us to the picnic."

Josias was certain that to Ivan it seemed incredibly logical. He supposed to any outsider it looked perfectly logical that he and Naomi might one day be more than…than… what they were now. But he knew the truth. He didn't want to get married again and certainly not to someone as restless as Naomi Ebersol.

"She did go with us to the picnic," Josias agreed. "And she is not my sister. But she and I haven't decided to get married. So no, she won't be your new *mamm*, either."

"Aww," Ivan groaned, and the rest of his brothers joined in. Even Tommy.

"That's too bad," Dale said. "Naomi would make a good *mamm*."

Chapter Nine

Naomi arrived early on Monday, fully expecting to get breakfast for everyone at the Schrock household. Instead, when she stepped inside the overly warm kitchen she was greeted with five less than happy boys sitting at the table with their not-so-happy father. The table was piled high with food, though Naomi was a little concerned that term was a bit too generous. A plate stacked high with nearly black toasted bread was set next to a bowl of runny eggs. She wasn't sure how it was possible, but even they appeared both undercooked and overcooked as well as rubbery. The platter with bacon was also an enigma. Half the bacon looked undercooked, and the other half perfectly matched the toast.

"Naomi!" The minute he laid eyes on her, Josias got to his feet as if he'd been doing something he wasn't supposed to. Which was ridiculous. He was sitting in his own house. She was the interloper.

"Good morning." She nodded at him, unsure at how to proceed. Which was also ridiculous. He was just a job. Engagement rumors aside, she was his nanny. There was nothing to be so awkward about. Yet there it remained, that awkwardness. It seemed to wind around them, intertwining everyone together. Or maybe it was just the two of them. The boys seemed overjoyed that she was there.

"Naomi! Naomi! Naomi!" They all jumped from their seats and danced around her.

"We're so glad you're here," Dale said. His grin was wide enough that she wasn't sure if he was excited to see her in general or because her arrival could potentially save them from having to eat that breakfast. For the time being anyway. It was a lot of food to go to waste. And they didn't waste food.

"Do you have pigs?" Naomi asked.

Josias frowned. "Like in the yard?"

Naomi chuckled. "That's where most people keep them," she said. But she wished she hadn't brought it up yet. She'd thought maybe Josias wouldn't feel quite so bad if she tossed his breakfast out to the hogs and made something fresh for them all. She'd gotten up extra early to make sure she had everything ready for the day but had skipped her breakfast at home because she knew she would be coming here. After one look at the meal piled up on the table, she was beginning to regret that decision.

"*Jah*," Josias said with a frown. "Why?"

Of course, she couldn't toss this breakfast out without making sure they had everything else they needed to make a new breakfast. She ignored his question and made her way to the refrigerator to check the contents inside. There were still a dozen eggs and half a block of cheese. Though there weren't any more packages of breakfast meat. She could improvise.

She turned and faced the group of men staring at her

as if she had appeared out of thin air. "Whose chore is it to feed the pigs?"

Dale's hand shot into the air, as well as Harley's.

"And whose job is it to feed the chickens?"

It was Ivan's turn to raise his hand. Since he was only about three, she figured that was correct.

She looked to Eli. "Do you have morning chores?"

He nodded. "I feed the dogs."

Okay," she said. "And who would like to have cinnamon biscuits for breakfast?" The four oldest boys shot their hands in the air, with Tommy following closely behind out of mimicry.

"You don't have—" Josias started but broke off when she shook her head at him. She was a little surprised when he backed down. She had walked in his house and taken over. But that was what he hired her for, and after looking at the breakfast he prepared, it was a good thing he had.

"Dale, you and Harley take those eggs and feed those to the hogs."

"*Jah*, okay," Dale said. "This is how we get cinnamon biscuits?"

Naomi nodded. "This is exactly how you get cinnamon biscuits." She turned to Ivan. "You take the toast out and crumble it up so the chickens can have it."

"Okay," he said.

"And Eli, you take the bacon out to the dogs."

That way no food would be technically wasted. Anything left could go to the hogs. Or perhaps Josias had a couple of goats out there. She hadn't noticed when she came in.

"*Jah*, Mamm," Eli said.

At first she thought no one had heard but her. The boys

went about their business, grabbing the food off the table and starting for the door, but when she turned to look at Josias, the expression on his face told her that he had heard as well.

Horror-struck. She had heard that word somewhere. She couldn't remember where. She'd never given it much thought. Maybe because she had never seen someone horror-struck before. But Josias Schrock was definitely struck with horror that Eli had called her *Mamm*.

"I—I—" Josias stumbled over whatever it was he was going to say. She was fairly certain it was an apology, but there was none needed.

"It's okay," she said. But that little slipup had done something to her heart. And she didn't understand what or why. Mattie's daughter had called her Mamm before on accident. Priscilla's two daughters called everybody mama, including their grandfather. So, it was a mystery why Eli Schrock's little slipup made her heart skip a beat and her stomach clench.

Because you know that'll never happen for you.

It was true. It might not ever be true for her that she would be a *mamm*, because when she got back from art school... Well, most of the unmarried men would already be married with children of their own. And though the Amish preached forgiveness, she worried how she would be perceived in the community after spending so much time away.

Everyone seemed to have accepted Samuel easily enough back into the community, but she knew for certain that it was different for men. Everything was, whether she liked it or not. Whether or not it was fair didn't matter. That was just the way it was.

"Did my breakfast look that bad?" Josias asked.

Naomi had been raised not to be unduly harsh. So, she gave him a small, encouraging smile. Then she looked into those blue-gray eyes and had to tell him the truth. "*Jah*. I'm sorry. It did."

"I didn't expect you to make every meal for us."

"But your sisters were doing that for you. And your *mamm*, right?"

His cheeks took on a small pink tinge, but he nodded. "*Jah*."

"And you hired me for the summer to fill in for them, correct?"

"Correct," he conceded.

"Then I'll come in the mornings and make breakfast. I'll make lunch, and then I'll cook you guys supper before I go home."

"You should have supper with us. You told me that you were going to talk to your family about it so they would expect you to be here for supper."

"Just today."

Josias shook his head. "The least you can do is eat here after you've already cooked. I'm sure your sisters are already cooking at home."

Jah, her sisters were cooking for themselves and their *dat* and the twins. Truth be known, it was tiring to leave after cooking only to go home and cook again. It only made sense that she eat there with Josias and the boys.

Like a wife would do.

She pushed the thought away. *Jah*, it was what a wife would do, but it was also what a full-time nanny would do as well. At least in her idea of what a full-time nanny should do.

"If you're sure it's not a burden. You know, on the budget." One more adult mouth to feed was a lot when you added three meals a day, five days a week.

"I think we can manage." Josias's lips quirked into a wry smile. "Plus, the boys love having you here."

"I like—I mean, they're great boys." She almost said that she liked being there. But that sounded a little too intimate. She was *only* their nanny. That was one thing she had to make sure she remembered. Every chance she got.

Come lunchtime, Josias was more than ready to head back to the house, and it had nothing to do with the fact that Naomi Ebersol would be waiting there. Though when he walked in the door he couldn't help but smile, knowing that she was there. But he quickly put the rein on that joy. She was his nanny. She would never be anything more to him because she was too much like Marie. And he couldn't let his heart go through that again. He never wanted to feel like he was keeping someone from what they truly wanted in life.

As he entered the kitchen there was a mad flurry of papers and all sorts of things shoved behind little backs and mostly out of his sight. All of his boys, even Tommy, wore strained grins that seemed to hide something. Though he wasn't sure what. He looked to Naomi.

Her smile was genuine, warm and sweet. But maybe she was just a better actor than his boys.

"What's going on?"

Naomi shook her head and looked down to the left. She

was lying. How he had picked up on this tell, he didn't know. But he knew that part for a fact. When she professed things that weren't true, she looked down and to the left. Then she looked back up and innocently met his gaze.

"I see," Josias said.

Naomi gave a small frown. As if she didn't understand the relevance of his response. She wasn't the only one who could be mysterious.

She smiled once more and headed toward him. Just before she reached his side, she shot a telling look at Dale and gave him a quick nod.

Something was definitely up. Though he figured it would be a while before he would find out what it was.

Naomi slipped her arm through his and spun him around toward the entryway to the kitchen. "I have a question to ask you about the washing machine," she said smoothly, leading him from the room and out onto the back porch.

They stopped in front of the machine and peered at it.

"What's your question?"

"Uh..." It seemed perhaps she hadn't thought this far in advance. "The detergent," she said brightly. And he had a feeling she hadn't been trying to do any laundry this morning. Whatever it was they had been working on in the kitchen had most probably used up all their time. In fact, he didn't see any lunch cooking on the stove, and he didn't smell any as he came into the house. So, chances were, the special project had also jeopardized a hot meal. No matter. It was getting too warm outside to eat anything cooked for lunch.

Josias moved toward the cabinet just to the left of the washing machine. He opened the door. "Everything you need should be right in here." He had detergent and bleach and even a small bottle of fabric softener.

"Good," she said. "I'm going to wash church clothes this afternoon."

She was stalling, that was what she was doing, holding him on the porch until the boys cleaned up whatever project they had going on in the kitchen. The question truly was why the project was a secret. But for now, he would let it slide. He trusted Naomi.

The thought was strange. He really didn't know her that well. Well, enough to trust her with his children. But he trusted her with more, it seemed.

Josias leaned back against the cabinet and crossed his arms. "You think it's safe to go back in?"

He had toyed with the idea of confronting her about her secrecy or letting it slide. But once he saw the bright rose color growing on her cheeks, he decided he'd made the right decision. The color was, as his *grossmammi* would say, very fetching.

"I don't know what you're talking about."

So that was how they were gonna play it. "If you say so."

"I do." She gave a firm nod of her chin, but he noticed she made no move to go back into the kitchen. They stood that way for a minute more, and suddenly Josias was overcome with the intimacy of the situation. Here he was on a small, narrow porch, mere inches, not even an arm's distance, from Naomi Ebersol. And there was no one else around.

And they were just waiting.

And there was a part of him—

"Naomi," Dale called from the doorway leading back into the house. "Tommy's hungry."

Her whole expression brightened, and for a moment he wondered if she had been feeling the same pull that he had felt, the unwanted attraction of one to the other.

"I guess it's time to feed the boys," she said, her voice just a little too high, a little too chipper. Then she spun on her heel and made her way back into the kitchen.

"What's for lunch?" he asked.

Naomi bit her lip, her expression turning just a bit sheepish. "I thought we would have sandwiches." She moved toward the bag she had brought in that morning and pulled a loaf of crusty bread from inside.

"I've been teaching my sister Sarah Ann to bake, and this is the latest batch of our sourdough bread."

"You baked the bread that we're going to have for sandwiches?" Josias knew a couple of women in their church district baked bread for every day, but most of the younger women preferred buying a loaf of bread from the store. Especially when the children started coming. There just wasn't enough time in the day to bake bread when a person had two in diapers and one on the way.

But that thought made him think of Naomi in that position. He felt his cheeks fill with heat, and he pushed the thought immediately away.

"I did. I enjoy baking."

"Yum," the boys chorused.

Somehow, when she said the words, he seemed to realize that he had heard that around somewhere. No telling where. In a community as small as theirs, word got around about everything. And after sampling her spur-of-the-moment cinnamon biscuits from that morning, he knew it to be a fact. Or if she didn't like it, she was definitely good at it.

She started giving the boys things to do, and he stood and watched for a moment. Why hadn't he thought of that? He engaged their help outside in feeding the animals and raking leaves and all the other chores, but he had never once thought for them to help him get their meals together. Just another thing that he could learn from Naomi Ebersol.

In no time at all, she had sandwiches, chips, pickles and all sorts of condiments on the table ready for them to eat. And the bread? So good he could hardly stand it.

"Are we having sandwiches for supper, too?" Dale asked.

Before Josias could answer, Naomi did. She laughed. "Of course not. Though I was thinking we might have spaghetti. If you like the bread, I have another loaf, and we can make garlic bread from that. What you think about that idea?"

He loved it. But Josias didn't say anything because she wasn't talking to him.

That was okay because Dale had enough enthusiasm for all six of them.

"*Jah!* Please!"

"Then it's a plan."

He thanked Naomi, then went back outside to work. Thankfully he was just working to repair a part of the hayloft that had rotted through. He had already fixed the leak in the roof that had caused that hole, and the construction work for it, other than the measuring, he could practically do in his sleep. Because all he could think about was Naomi inside with his boys. Not that he was worried. That was one thing that wasn't happening. He trusted her completely with his children. No, he couldn't help but think about their secret project. Were they still working on it? Or had they wrapped it up for the day?

And spaghetti. He loved spaghetti. And the thought of that sourdough bread she had baked smothered in butter and garlic made his mouth water even though he was still stuffed from lunch. Most of all, he was so glad that she was going to be there when he got in from his work. And she would eat supper with them tonight and come back in the morning and make breakfast and they would start it all over again. He shouldn't be as happy with that idea as he was—but he was.

"Just leave those," Josias said with a quick nod toward the supper dishes. "You should be getting home before it gets too late."

"I appreciate that," Naomi said. And she did, but she couldn't leave the dinner dishes for him to take care of. "It will be light for another two hours," she said.

She was exaggerating a bit, maybe an hour and a half, an hour and fifteen minutes, but tonight she was not going to leave the dinner dishes for him to do after all the work he had done that day and the fact that he still had to give the boys their baths. They had decided at some point that that was the best way to go. Yes, she was there to help him with the boys, but if she cooked all the meals, cleaned the house, did the laundry and was there if the boys needed her, then he would take care of them in the evenings. And it was true that this was the first full day she had spent with them and perhaps their rhythm would change as time went on, but they needed to try their agreed-upon schedule first to see if it worked.

"It just seems like a lot," Josias said. "You cooked and cleaned all day."

She shot him a smile that was half wonderment and half disbelief. "Isn't that what you're paying me to do?"

He opened his mouth once, then closed it. Then he opened it once more but stuttered as he spoke. "Well, *jah*. But you've been here all day and I just—"

"And you worked on the farm all day."

He shook his head, and she wondered if he had done this with his wife. But she knew he hadn't. They had their roles, and she, Naomi, was not his wife.

She tossed down the dishrag and turned to face him. "Are you going do this every day? Because if you are, it's going to be a long summer."

She didn't know why he was being so stubborn. He had hired her to do a job, and she surely couldn't take his money if she only did half of it. And then when she got to art school—

She slammed her thoughts down. She wasn't going to think about art school. Not just yet. Because every time she began to think about leaving, even to do something as glorious as learning to draw and paint, the idea filled her with trepidation. Worry. Doubt.

He shook his head. "I just don't want to feel like I'm taking advantage. You're working so hard."

"I don't feel like you're taking advantage." And she had been working hard. But she had enjoyed every minute of it. She always heard that boys and girls were different in their mannerisms and attitudes, but she never had an opportunity to experience it. And though Mattie's daughters weren't as active or quite as inquisitive as the boys, she found the boys' enthusiasm for life to be engaging. And somehow, their awe and wonder seemed to foster her own. "Let's make a deal," she said. "If I feel like I'm being taken advantage of I promise to tell you immediately. Is that okay?"

He nodded.

"In turn you let me do what you're paying me to do for you. Okay?"

He hesitated for a split second. Such a brief span of time that she wondered if he even noticed. She did. So why was he so reluctant to turn over care to her? He thought she was going to break his dishes? Doubtful. No, she had a feeling Josias Schrock had a few more reasons why he had trouble letting go.

Chapter Ten

"Are you going to be our new *mamm*?"

Eli's so innocently asked question took her breath away.

She had the boys sitting at the table working on the rest of the surprise for Josias's birthday. Dale had told her that his birthday was coming up on Thursday, so she only had two more days to get everything ready.

They had started with birthday cards, just a simple folded piece of paper decorated by each boy, but that didn't seem like enough. Now she had them sitting at the table with fingerpaints. She tried to tell herself that anyone would've done the same, but she knew it was her artistic side that brought out this addition. But how fun would it be to have a picture painted by each one of his sons hanging on the wall? She had even given one to Tommy. Though she was glad the paint was washable and nontoxic. So far, he'd gotten more of it in his hair than he had on the paper, but he was having a really good time. His brothers were as well. So much so that she decided she was going to paint one herself.

But her fingers stilled as Eli looked at her plainly, waiting for her answer.

"She's not going to be our new *mamm*," Dale said. "Dat said."

"Nuh-uh," Eli countered. "He said she could be."

"But not that she was *going* to be." Dale glared at Eli, but Eli wasn't budging.

"That means she can be."

Like it or not, it was time to step in. Naomi cleared her throat, then grabbed a paper towel and wiped her fingers clean. "I think you boys are wonderful. And I'm going to so enjoy spending the summer with you, but I'm sorry. I will not become your new *mamm*." Those words shouldn't have stuck in her throat, but she barely got them out. Why was she so choked up? She wouldn't be their *mamm*, she was going to art school, and even if she wasn't going to art school, she wouldn't be their *mamm*.

"Aww," Eli said, dropping his head down so the tips of his blond hair rubbed in the blue paint on his paper.

"I'm sorry to disappoint you," Naomi said, hating the fact that she herself seemed a little disappointed at the prospect. "But you need to watch your hair in the paint."

"Sorry," Eli said, the word lisped out from the hole where his two front teeth should've been.

"It's okay," she said. "Are you finished?"

She had already decided to move everybody's painting out to the buggy. She would secure them with little stones in each corner and allow them to dry. Surely Josias wouldn't be looking in her buggy anytime today, and he wouldn't see the five beautiful paintings his sons had made.

"I guess so." Eli's lower lip stuck out just a bit.

"There's still time if you want to paint more. Or if you're really done with your painting you can help me work on the sign."

"Are you finished with your painting?" Dale asked with a small nod toward her own paper.

She looked down at what she had painted. Just blue ocean with a slightly lighter blue on top for the sky. Shadows of dark blue green inside represented a few small fish. Or maybe they were very large fish, very far away. That was something she wanted left up to the viewer.

"I'm finished." Harley screwed up his face and stared at her painting. "It's blue."

She smiled at him. "That it is."

"It looks like Tommy's," Eli said.

Naomi glanced over to where Tommy was still smearing his hands happily across his paper. Whereas hers was blue, his was purple, though there were a few streaks of red and blue that hadn't managed to get smeared together to make the beautiful royal color. But not many. Yet the love with which he produced the painting was something she could see immediately and knew that Josias would be able to see, too. In fact, she was fairly certain that a father's eyes looking at these pictures his sons had drawn would experience a joy and an insight that only a father could feel.

"I think he's done, too."

She took his painting away despite his fussing and began to wipe off his hands with the wet rag. She was going to have to dump them in the bathtub to get all the purple off them, but it would be worth it in the end.

"As you boys get finished, go ahead and start working on the sign. I've outlined a few things you can paint in the lines. Or you can do anything you want outside the lines, okay? But if you're going to paint in the lines where there are words, be sure to paint in the lines—got it?"

"Got it," they all said.

She scooped Tommy up into her arms, then dabbed one hand back into the paint on his tray. She walked him over to the large swatch of butcher paper she had spread out on the floor. She tipped him over headfirst and placed his hand gently on the corner of the paper.

"What are you doing?" Dale asked.

"We're signing the picture. This one, at least. That way your *dat* can see how big your handprints are now and compare them later, after you are all grown up." Josias could look back and remember when they were this little. It wasn't a present that could be fully realized for years to come, but she was glad she had thought of it.

"As everybody gets finished, I want you to do one handprint in the corner and then begin painting the rest, okay? And be sure to remember which one is yours. I don't care what color you use, just remember what color it is so I can write your name next to them, so your father will know what handprint belongs to what boy."

Dale held up one hand, splaying his fingers out as wide as possible. "He'll know which hand is mine because mine will be the biggest. Because I'm the oldest."

"No doubt," Naomi said.

Eli jumped to his feet. "Mine's next."

Naomi shook her head at the boys as they began to chatter about whose hand should be where, whose was biggest, and when they would grow, and all the other things that brothers seemed to be competitive about. She took Tommy to the bathroom to get the purple paint off him before his father came into the house and the surprise was ruined.

But as she washed the little boy's hair, all she could think about was Eli asking, *Are you going to be our new* mamm?

Thursday was just one of those days where nothing went right. His buggy horse threw a shoe, and the container of pesticide that he just bought was empty, making him wonder if he'd dreamed the whole thing. That was the only option other than somebody sneaking onto his property, stealing the pesticide out of the container and leaving it behind. Which made no sense at all. At any rate, it was gone and he needed more, but he couldn't get to town because his pony only had three shoes. He cut his hand, hit his elbow and twisted his knee trying to walk over the tree roots.

Some days it just didn't pay to get out of bed. And today was his birthday. Not that he expected anyone to say anything or do anything. His family wasn't like that. A birthday sometimes would come and go years at a time before they would have any sort of acknowledgment, and that was okay. He didn't need constant attention, but for some reason today he just felt old.

He shouldn't. He was only twenty-eight today. It wasn't like thirty or forty or some milestone birthday that people tended to over celebrate.

Twenty-eight. He never imagined he'd be twenty-eight, much less a widowed single *dat* with five boys. He just never thought...

It had been a busy day as well, and now that he had to go into town and buy more pesticide this afternoon, it was making it busier still. But he was excited about one thing. Going in and eating lunch with his family. It'd been a long time since he had been able to enjoy such a simple pleasure.

Not even taking into account the months that Marie had been gone. There were the months before where she had been ill. Unable to get out of bed. Unable to lift her head. Overwhelmed with grief, then overwhelmed with being overwhelmed. It wasn't their way. All things were up to God and God's will was accepted. And for the most part they all did just that: accept God's will. But he knew now, firsthand, that wasn't always an easy thing to do.

He didn't want to think about Annabelle. Not today. He was sad enough, weary enough already. He didn't need to add that sinking grief on top of it all. He was going in to have lunch with his family and Naomi. And he was looking forward to it.

He stepped into the back door of the house and stopped just inside at the sink he had installed a couple of years ago. With farming, you never knew how dirty you were going to be coming in, and he hated coming in with the unspeakable all over his hands then walking to the kitchen sink and washing them there. No, it was much better to wash them out here, take off his boots and then head into the house proper. And that was just what he did.

"Surprise!"

Josias stopped, looking around in disbelief. They were all there, his kids, and Naomi, too. Standing under a sign that said Happy Birthday, Dat. The sign was decorated with all sorts of drawings, some discernible, some not, with a trail of handprints on one side. He could just make out each name below the impression. A record of how big they were on this day.

"Happy birthday," Naomi said.

"Thank you," he managed to choke out. Tears prickled

at the back of his eyes. Tears of joy and thankfulness and just the overwhelming feeling of being loved. And suddenly that drag of age was lifted.

"We made you a cake," Harley said, jumping up and down.

Josias looked over to the table where a casual meal had been laid out. Cold cut sandwiches on more of Naomi's wonderful sourdough bread and a cake that looked a little lopsided—or maybe that was the frosting. Ripe red strawberries had been placed all around the edges.

"Good," Josias said. "I'm hungry and it looks good."

Naomi shook her head. "Oh no, you don't. Sandwiches first."

The boys groaned their displeasure, and they dragged their feet as they made their way to their chairs.

Everyone sat, and Josias bowed his head for the prayer. He thanked God for the food, the weather, his beautiful family. *And thank you, Lord, for bringing Naomi to us. I know I won't have her here long. But please, Lord, make sure I appreciate her for the time that she is. Amen.*

Apparently, the boys had been painting on something or another all week, though he wasn't sure exactly what. They were telling the anecdotes of their week, the words spewing from them like water from a fire hydrant. He supposed all that excitement had been kept bottled up for days, and now that they could let it loose, it was everywhere. He let them talk, hardly understanding half of what they said but trying his best to anyway. He figured Naomi would give him the particulars when the time came. For now, he was just going to enjoy their effusive excitement. Once the meal was complete, Naomi got a single candle and stuck it in the center of his cake.

"I didn't know how old you were today so..." She pointed to the single candle.

"Twenty-eight," he told her.

His sons' eyes bugged out and their mouths popped open like he was older than Methuselah.

"Well, this year you only have the one candle to blow out."

"Thank goodness," he said with a small chuckle.

Naomi lit the candle, and she and the boys all began to sing happy birthday to him. He couldn't remember the last time someone had made this big of a deal out of his birthday. Probably right before he and Marie got married. Seven, eight years ago at least.

Once they finished singing, he closed his eyes and made his wish. Then he blew out the candle.

"What you wish for?" Harley asked as Naomi cut them slices of the cake. It was a yellow butter cake with buttercream frosting and strawberries for garnish. His absolute favorite, and he wondered how Naomi knew. The chances of her getting that correct, without any help from his family, were too slim for her not to have been in contact with someone whose last name was Schrock. The thought that she went to all that trouble had his insides feeling all warm and soft, like a gooey marshmallow over a campfire. And the worst part of it all was that he didn't hate it.

"I can't tell you what I wished for, or it won't come true." He wasn't sure on that one, but he sure wasn't telling anyone what he had prayed for. Because there was a small, small part of him that both wished and prayed that

Naomi Ebersol would change her mind about going to art school and would instead continue to stay there in Millers Creek. Continue to be his nanny, making sure each and every one of their birthdays was celebrated to the fullest extent. And possibly something other than just his nanny. A friend. Maybe even more...

The thought twisted his stomach into a hard knot. It was slightly terrifying. And wonderful. And beautiful. All at the same time.

"I know that you have to get back to work," Naomi started. "But we have a few little things for you."

The boys all finished their cake and slid out of their chairs. They dutifully marched over to the wall next to the pantry. He had noticed them there when he had first come in, several picture frames all turned backward where whatever was inside wasn't showing. But at the time, he hadn't been able to give it much thought. Now each boy grabbed one and came back to the table. Yep. Naomi was definitely behind this. One hundred percent.

"We all painted you a picture," she said. "Not like paint paint, but finger painted, and I figured that was okay." She was beginning to stumble over her words, and he wondered if there was something in his expression that made her think that he was angry. He wasn't angry; he was stunned. No one, *no one*, had ever done this for him.

One by one, the boys brought the pictures over to him, each explaining what it was they had painted there. All except for Tommy, whose paper was mostly purple and somehow beautiful in its simplicity.

"And this is mine."

Her hands shook just a bit as she handed him the framed picture.

"It's blue," Dale told him.

"*Danki*," Josias drily replied.

It was blue, but once he began to look at it he could see the differences. He could see where the blue of the sky became the blue of water and the dark shapes hiding within that made—

"The ocean?" He had never seen the ocean, but he wanted to. He had heard tales of Pinecraft, Florida, and the Amish settlement there. He had been told of all the things a person could see when they went out in the water with a mask and a snorkel. He just couldn't imagine the wonders under the waves. But how he wanted to see it someday.

"*Jah*," she said, her voice quiet. "I think the ocean is just so incredible, and one day I hope to go see it."

"You've never been?" he asked, trying not to be stunned that they each had a common goal.

"No," she said simply.

He almost said, *We should go sometime.* But there was no *we* or *sometime* in a scenario where he and Naomi could travel to the ocean together.

"One day, though," she said. "One day." And he prayed like everything that she would make it there sooner rather than later.

"*Danki*," he said, looking at each one of them in turn. "Thank you so much. It was a wonderful birthday." So wonderful he hated the thought of getting up and going back outside to work. He wanted to stay in the house with them and see what they were going to do next. But farming never stopped, and he had been inside twice as long for this lunch than he was for his usual lunches. At this rate, it wouldn't be long before he needed to go out and milk the cows again. But if only he could stay...

A horn sounded outside.

"And that will be the milk truck driver coming to pick up today's load," he said, finally pushing himself to his feet.

If only...

Chapter Eleven

She thought he liked it. He seemed to like it. He smiled as he looked at all their pictures and paintings, and he had eaten two pieces of cake. She had brought another loaf of bread for him to have in case he got hungry for some midnight snack. Though she realized it was a little bit of overkill. She would be back tomorrow, but she wanted his birthday to be the best day possible.

Which was why she made meat loaf for supper with mashed potatoes and her special homemade sauce for the top. Esther had told Naomi that it was Josias's favorite meal. Which was perfect. Because, not to brag or anything, but her meat loaf was the best in the valley.

It was a hit with everyone, just as she knew it would be. Another round of birthday cake and they polished off the rest. Maybe tomorrow she would make a regular cake for them. Or a pie.

For now, she was ready to head home. It was a busy and exhausting day. She just had to wait a few more minutes for the boys to finish drying the dishes so she could stack them in the cabinet.

"If you want to go ahead and go," Josias said, "I can put the dishes away."

"Oh no," she protested. "It's your birthday. You shouldn't have to put dishes away on your birthday."

"But it's okay to milk a herd of fifty cows. Twice."

"That's different. That's *your* job. Putting dishes away is mine."

"Seriously," he said. "You look dead on your feet. Go get some rest. I promise I'll leave all the dishes out on the counter, and you can put them up yourself tomorrow. How's that?"

"Are you trying to get rid of me, Josias Schrock?"

"Absolutely," he said with a grin. "I hid one last piece of birthday cake, and until I get the boys in bed and you gone, I can't take it out of its hiding place."

"If I hadn't served all the cake myself, I would think you were telling the truth."

He laughed, and she loved the sound, absolutely loved it. She had noticed that he smiled a lot and laughed a lot, too. But for the most part the action seemed forced, the laughter just a little hollow. But his laugh now... It filled the room and lifted her spirits. And she had a feeling that he was happier now. She would like to think that she had a hand in that. Maybe just lifting some of the responsibility off him was enough. But she loved that she had a hand in this man's smile and full-bodied laugh.

"Seriously," he said. "Go. The boys and I can handle it."

As if they had practiced the move beforehand, Josias nodded, and Dale fetched a milk crate from the mudroom. Eli shifted the stool the siblings stood on to wash their hands so it was underneath the cabinet where the plates were stored.

She thought about it for a minute more then decided it

wasn't worth the arguing back and forth. It was just a load of dishes. And the boys seemed to have it handled just fine.

So, she said goodbye and started for the door.

"Keep that going," Josias said to his sons. "I'll be back in a minute." Then to Naomi's surprise he stepped outside with her.

"Where you going?" she asked. He was probably going out to sneak a smoke or something. She knew a lot of men who liked a tobacco pipe every now and then but didn't dare smoke in the house. Her father was one of these. But Josias just smiled at her in the waning light and whistled for her horse. The beast came running to the gate of the corral.

"Nice trick," she said.

He smiled. "You should see how it works on little boys." Then he led the horse from the paddock and began hitching her to Naomi's buggy.

"Thank you again," he said. "This is the best birthday I can ever remember."

Her cheeks flamed. She had wanted it to be the best birthday ever, but to hear him say that it actually was the best filled her with a supreme joy and a sense of accomplishment. On top of it all, she got to share her love of art and painting with the boys. It might be the best birthday that he could remember, but it was a really good day for her as well.

"I was happy to do it." She moved toward the opening of the buggy then turned, surprised to find him so close behind her. Not that it mattered. But with him that near she could see every little dark blue speck in his gray eyes. The tiny scar under one eye that looked like he'd been poked too hard with somebody's fingernail. She could even see something in his expression that she was afraid to name.

Mostly because she had a terrible feeling it was reflected in her own. Longing.

"Josias..." Her voice was breathy and quiet, too serious for a celebration, but all she could manage.

"Naomi," he said in return. But his tone wasn't joking, and his eyes seemed to burn through the falling night.

Somehow, she knew. He was about to kiss her. She could almost feel his intent, the nameless emotion that was pushing them together.

She stepped a little closer. It might be her one chance. Her one time before she left.

He came toward her slowly as if he were allowing her time to change her mind. Or maybe he was hoping he would change his. This wasn't allowed. They weren't actually engaged. They were employee and employer. Only friends helping each other for a short period to time. And yet...

She breathed in the heady scent of him—man, detergent, farm—and her stomach panged with something she dared not name. His lips were only inches from hers. A stolen kiss. That was what this would be. A willing kiss. A *verboten* kiss.

"Dat!"

They jumped apart, nearly banging heads in their haste to get away from one another before Harley noticed.

He had come out onto the porch and waited until he had his father's attention. "Dale said I had to get in the bath. I don't have to, right?"

"Of course you do." Josias sounded like someone had their hands wrapped around his neck. He cleared his throat. "Go back in the house. I'll be there in a minute."

"Okay." Harley sounded like he wanted to do anything but return to his bossy brother.

Naomi held her breath, as Josias waited for Harley to go back into the house. He turned his attention to her once again, and she could see it there on his face, the apology. But she didn't want him to be sorry for almost kissing her. They had both been just a little bit swept up in the setting sun and celebration of the day and the fact that they had been working together like a family for the entire week. She didn't want to hear that he was sorry about that because it would make the one thing that she didn't want to hear be the truth: he was still in love with Marie.

"Happy birthday, Josias," she said before he could get a word in. Then she swung up into her buggy and set the horse into motion. She wasn't sure, but she thought she heard him call a farewell as she drove away.

It was the longest ride home she had ever experienced. Somehow, she managed to keep her tumbling thoughts confined to things like whether or not Josias would want the leftover meat loaf tomorrow as a sandwich. And if she did make that for his lunch, what would the rest of them eat? Finally she pulled up into the driveway at her own house. Yet to her dismay, Priscilla was out on the front porch, as if waiting for her to come home.

"Hey," her twin called as she came toward Naomi. Without saying anything else, she started helping unhitch the horse from the buggy.

"Where are the girls?" Naomi asked.

Priscilla flipped one hand over her shoulder toward the house. "Inside with Dawdi."

Ever since Priscilla had given birth to her baby girl twins, she had referred to their father as Dawdi. Naomi supposed that was just how it went when you had children.

Not that she would know. Or even would in the future. She had thought about it long and hard. If she went off to art school in the fall, she would most likely cut her chances of getting married by 75 percent. She wasn't sure exactly how she came up with that math, but she figured at least half the men her age would be married when she returned, and if they weren't, she might not want to marry them at all to begin with. It was something she hadn't thought about when she applied to art school, and now she was beginning to have her doubts. And yet she still wanted to paint, to create, to reproduce the beautiful images she saw in her head so others might enjoy them as well. Was there really anything wrong with that?

"You're awfully quiet tonight," Priscilla said. She started toward the barn with the horse as Naomi pushed the carriage back into its spot under the barn eaves.

"I just got some things on my mind," Naomi said as she followed Priscilla into the barn. Her twin looped the reins around the nearest pole and started brushing the mare.

That was the truth. Naomi had a lot of things on her mind, including the almost kiss she had almost shared with Josias.

It was better this way, she told herself. Better that he hadn't kissed her. It was too forward of a move, for one. And he would regret it if he truly was still in love with Marie. And she had no reason to believe anything to the contrary.

"Like art school?" Priscilla's words were quietly spoken but fell heavy onto Naomi's heart.

"Evie told you."

Priscilla whirled on her then, grooming brush still in hand. "*Jah*, Evie told me. But I would've thought you would have."

"I didn't mean—" Naomi shook her head and started

again. "Evie found out by accident. She wasn't supposed to know at all. No one is supposed to know."

"Are you seriously thinking about going?"

"*Jah*," Naomi said, unwilling to tell more lies than necessary. "I wouldn't have applied if I didn't want to go." And the truth was, she had done much more than apply. She had studied for years in order to get her GED, because she had to have that before she could apply to the university. She had rented a post office box to hide her mail. This wasn't a spur-of-the-moment decision. It was something she had wanted almost as long as she could remember.

"I really wish you would've told me about this. Not had me find out from one of our sisters."

The pain in her voice was almost more than Naomi could take. She never meant to hurt Priscilla. They might not be the closest of the sisters, even though they were twins, but she loved Priscilla with all her heart.

"So, what is this engagement with Josias about then?"

Naomi shook her head. "Something he came up with. He said he thought it would distract Evie and the family. He was only trying to help."

Priscilla's face wrinkled into a scowling frown. "That is the dumbest thing I've ever heard. Why would he say something like that?"

"I have no idea." She had no idea why he did anything that he did. He was a perfect mystery to her, an enigma.

"He's not taking advantage of you, is he?" Priscilla's question was quietly asked but still echoed inside Naomi's thoughts.

"No. No, no, no," she said, shaking her head the whole time. He wasn't taking advantage of her but tonight he almost had. Or maybe she was taking advantage of him. She had taken that first step closer. It was all so very confusing.

"What happened?" Priscilla asked. She turned back to brushing down the mare.

"Nothing," Naomi said. It was the truth, but Priscilla could hear something in her tone, a loneliness maybe.

"What *almost* happened?" Apparently, her sister was too intuitive for her own good. Though she continued to groom the mare waiting for Naomi to answer.

"He almost kissed me."

Priscilla stopped brushing the horse and turned back to face her. "Sister...that is bad."

Finally, the tears she had known were coming eventually rose in her eyes. "This is not the worst part."

"It's not?"

"He hired me because he never wants to get married again. We were running around all day, it's his birthday, you know, and just acting like a family until I got ready to leave and then—well, I—"

Naomi managed to blink back all but one of the tears. It rolled down her cheek. She wiped it away with the back of her hand. It shouldn't matter to her one way or the other. She was leaving in less than three months. She was going to art school. Somehow, someway.

"Don't go back over there," Priscilla said quietly.

"I have to. I made an agreement with him."

"You can break it."

Naomi shook her head. "If I'm going to art school, I'm going to have to have money."

Priscilla led the horse to her usual stall, made sure she had clean hay and water, then came back to stare sadly at

Naomi. "And to think an hour ago I was just worried about you going to art school."

"Why are you worried?" Naomi asked.

"Let's see," she said, ticking off on her fingers. "You're my sister. I'm going to miss you. Things will not be the same around here without you. And you'll never come back." That was when her tough as nails sister started tearing up. Naomi hadn't seen Priscilla cry since they buried her husband, Mark.

"Of course I'm coming back." She moved to wrap her sister in a tight hug.

Priscilla squeezed her back, holding her so close they both shook.

"It's dangerous out there," Priscilla said. Finally, she pulled away, looking deep into Naomi's eyes. "Why do you have to go to school to draw? Can't you do that anywhere?"

"It's not the same," Naomi said. "They'll teach me techniques and colors and things like that." Actually, she'd never really thought about it. Somehow along the way, she had got it into her head that it was what she needed to do.

"You're smart. You could check out books from the library and learn it that way."

"*Jah*, Dat would really go for that."

"Like he's going to go for you leaving for art school."

It was a valid point, but one that Naomi didn't want to address.

"You've been drawing and doing all sorts of things on the sly for a decade at least, why can't you continue to do that?"

Chapter Twelve

Why *couldn't* she continue to do that? Naomi didn't have the answer for her sister.

Priscilla waited patiently, but no words came for Naomi to explain.

Finally, Priscilla continued, "All our lives we have been different than other twins, I know that. You know that. We're competitive and opposing. Sometimes I feel like we spend our whole lives doing our best to be opposite from each other."

Naomi had felt it, too, but she attributed most of that to Priscilla's personality and not her own. So having her sister say it made her realize that *jah*, there had been times when she had made her choice based off what Priscilla wouldn't do.

"It doesn't have to be that way. Please, don't go off to the English world just to be different. It's not worth it."

Was that what she was doing? Going off to learn to draw so she could be as different from Priscilla as possible? What did it even matter anymore? When they were younger, some of it had been to get their *dat*'s attention, especially after losing their *mamm* at such a young age. Frankly, she wasn't proud of a lot of her behavior shortly after Grace Ann Ebersol died. But what was done was done, and forgiveness flowed freely in their family.

But Priscilla's words made her think of the one question that plagued her the most. What if she went to school and came back unhappy? Came back unsatisfied with the life she left behind. A person just had to look at Helen Schrock to see that going off could be a very, very bad idea. And Helen didn't even leave the Amish community.

What if Naomi left and couldn't come back? Would drawing be worth it then?

"Just think about it," Priscilla begged. "Promise me you'll think about it."

Naomi swallowed hard and gave her sister one last squeeze. "I promise."

Truth be told, it was all that Naomi *could* think about. When she went to Josias's house on Friday, he acted like nothing had happened between them. And truthfully, nothing had. So, she went along, doing her best to forget all about it. She baked bread. She baked cake. She even made them a pie for the weekend.

She spent Saturday doing her own laundry, helping clean the house, and otherwise playing with Priscilla's little girls. Naomi had never felt closer to Priscilla than she did then. That in itself was confusing enough to make her doubt going away for any amount of time. Perhaps the relationship between her and her sister could be different from this point forward.

Naomi had never really thought about it, but she was certain that losing her husband at such a very young age had to have a dramatic effect on Priscilla. But Priscilla didn't turn to Naomi for comfort. She had Lizzie and Sarah Ann flocking around her, doing her every bidding. Then Mattie lost her husband and Naomi and Evie camped with her. She'd never realized it before, but those two deaths had split the Ebersol sisters down the middle, with Priscilla and Naomi landing on different sides.

"Are you going with us?" Priscilla asked, stopping by Naomi's room Sunday morning after breakfast.

Naomi was pretending to read, though truly she was stewing on the decisions she was about to make. "Where you going?"

"We're going over to see Mattie and the girls."

It was typical for a non-church Sunday. Everybody wanted to visit, and everybody was taking it easy since it was the Lord's Day. After her talk with Priscilla on Thursday night, Naomi thought it would be a great idea if all the sisters could get together.

"Let me get my shoes," Naomi said, reaching for the black slip-ons she had tucked under the edge of her bed.

Priscilla rolled her eyes. "Shoes. Fancy girl."

Naomi laughed and followed her sister out the door, down the stairs and into the waiting buggy.

Mattie was excited to see all her sisters together, and the Ebersol girls found lawn chairs in the shed and pulled them into the shade of a large tree that sat off to one side of Mattie's house. They lined their chairs into a circle and put the girls in the center so they could all play together. Mattie even dragged the kitchen play set out for them to bang around on.

The sisters all sat around together, knees touching, the

next generation playing in front of them as they laughed and visited.

"I can't remember the last time we got together like this," Sarah Ann said.

"It's not been that long ago," Mattie protested. "We were together at my wedding."

"That doesn't count," Lizzie admonished.

"Why not?" Mattie gave her sister a mock pout.

But Naomi missed the reason why Mattie's wedding didn't count as a sisters' get-together. Just the mention of the wedding brought back thoughts of Josias. Naomi had never really talked to him before that moment. Only knew him in passing. Now look at them. Rumored to be engaged. Almost kissing. Maybe even…

She pushed the thought away. She was not falling in love with Josias Schrock. No matter that he was a good father, trying his best at every turn, failing most times but trudging on. It didn't matter that he thought she might be the best baker in all of Millers Creek or that he came to her rescue when he deemed that she needed rescuing. Though truth be told, she wasn't sure how she would have gotten out of telling her family about art school. And she was going to have to tell them eventually. So, the question remained… Why had she let him talk her into becoming his nanny for the summer?

"Naomi!" Mattie shrieked.

Jarred out of her thoughts, Naomi jumped to her feet. "What?"

"Art school?" Mattie said accusingly.

Naomi's gaze swung from Evie to Priscilla, and she knew instantly that her twin was the one to spill the beans. No doubt to get their sisters on her side in talking Naomi out of going away.

"You can't go away," Sarah Ann said.

"You can't go to school," Lizzie added.

"What will everyone say?" Sarah Ann continued.

"What will the bishop say?" Evie asked.

"What will Dat say?" Mattie muttered. And in that moment Naomi knew the biggest hurt of all would be dealt to their father. Was she ready for that? Was she ready to break his heart?

"I'm coming back," she said, sitting back down and doing her best not to let the trembling in her hands show. This moment had been building. She knew that it was coming. Not that it made it any easier. And she still had her father to contend with. But she didn't want everyone knowing because she didn't want to have to defend her decision over and over again for months before she left. That sort of tension would drain all the fun out of the adventure that awaited her.

"You don't know that," Priscilla said wisely.

Naomi hated the words her sister said. Hated their truth. She didn't know if she was coming back. She only knew that she intended to return.

"Helen Schrock was coming back," Lizzie pointed out.

"She did come back," Naomi protested, but even to her own ears, her words sounded weak and unsure.

"Only to leave again."

"I know something." Sarah Ann squirmed in her seat.

"What?" Lizzie demanded to know.

"I heard that Helen Schrock is having a baby. That's why she left to go to New Wilmington."

A few sad gasps went up among the sisters, right in tune with the sad shake of their heads.

"She didn't even go to the English world," Lizzie said, wide-eyed.

"She might as well have," Evie said.

"So, it's true?" Priscilla asked.

If anyone would know, it was Evie, seeing as how her fiancé had once been engaged to Helen, before she had decided to spend some time in Lancaster County with her fancy cousins.

Evie slowly nodded.

"Why didn't you tell us?" Lizzie squeaked.

Evie shook her head. "I didn't want to spread gossip, and I figured it wouldn't be long before everyone knew anyhow."

"Then she left."

"Right," Evie continued.

"And I'm too busy planning my wedding to give anything else much thought." Lizzie tossed her prayer *kapp* strings over her shoulder and shook them.

"Stop," Evie countered, though they all knew Lizzie was teasing. Everyone was so very happy that Evie had found her love.

It had been impossible for them not to see that Evie had been in love with Freeman since they were kids, but of course Freeman never realized it. But now the two had found their way to each other and life was sweet. Blessed.

But art school. That was where Naomi's happiness lay. She just knew it. Had known it for years, so many that she had been preparing for this practically her entire adult life.

Just when Naomi thought they would stop talking about her, Mattie turned to her once more.

"It's going to be so hard out there for you. Are you sure you're ready for that?"

"Of course I am." But was she?

She hadn't given any thought to how she was going to get around in Philadelphia. Probably by bus or walking. She still had to contact the school about living arrangements, but she also knew there were bigger problems that had to be addressed.

"What about church?" Mattie asked.

Leave it to the oldest of them to direct their conversation to the heart of the matter. Church. Church was so very important to them all. Their lives revolved around the church. Where a person lived determined who was in their church district. Everybody in the church district were the people that they went to school with, their closest neighbors, their closest friends. And it was all intertwined with the places they shopped. But she was going to break away from that. And she could survive it all except...

"You'll need to do something," Mattie said.

"Please, do something," Sarah Ann pleaded.

"I was thinking maybe I would try to find a Mennonite church there." Though she had a feeling they would be vastly different than the Old Order Mennonites they had in the valley. But she could hope that they would allow her in and keep her soul safe when she was out in the world.

"That'll be different," Priscilla said.

Naomi couldn't tell if she was being sarcastic or helpful. From the concern she saw on her twin's face, she decided it was helpful.

"I know, but I figured they would be the closest to what I have right now."

And she knew that wasn't very close at all. But at least most of the women there covered their hair. That was something she had heard, anyway. And she knew she would stick out like a sore thumb. But that was the cost of what she was doing.

"They will not dress the same," Lizzie said.

Sarah Ann's mouth fell open as if Lizzie had said the unthinkable. She snapped it shut then turned to Naomi. "You have English clothes?"

Naomi shook her head. "I think you guys don't understand. I'm just going to learn to draw. I'm coming back. I'm not turning English, and I don't have any English clothes." She couldn't imagine putting anything else on her body than the dresses that she and her sisters made for one another—conservative style, muted colors, wholesome, godly. She wouldn't be running around in blue jeans or those tight silky pants that all the English women seemed to wear these days. She would wear her regular shoes, her regular clothes and her prayer *kapp*. And *jah*, she would stick out like a Jersey cow in a field of Holsteins. That wasn't the point. She was only going there to learn to draw.

"I don't think that will work," Mattie said. "What if you can't find a Mennonite church? What if everyone makes fun of you?"

"What if you hate it there?" Sarah Ann completely nailed Naomi's biggest concern. The concern that she pushed way down deep inside. The concern that rose to the surface every night when she was alone in her room. What if she hated it? She always told herself that she would come back early. She could leave whenever she wanted to.

But she also knew that she was stubborn, and she had planned this for so long that it wouldn't be easy to walk away, even if she found herself homesick, lonesome, outcast and sad. And every night she prayed that when the time came, *if* the time came, that God would help her through her stubbornness. He would direct her steps back home.

But deep inside the doubt remained. And if she was leaving her church behind, would God be able to hear her there? Would He answer her call if she had walked away?

"If that happens, I'll just come home." Naomi was proud of the confidence and surety she heard in her own voice. Yet doubts remained. Once she left and came back, nothing would ever be the same, and she had to wonder if drawing was going to be worth it.

For Josias, non-church Sundays represented time to reflect and visit with his family. Normally, that was to say, when his mother and sister were home, he packed up his boys and went to his parents' house. And since it was a lot easier to travel three adults than one man and five rowdy boys, his father, his brother Levi and his sister Esther all came for supper on Sunday night.

He was just pulling the casserole that Naomi had put together for them on Friday from the oven when his sister found her way into the kitchen.

"Something smells good," Esther said.

"*Danki*," Josias replied. "Though I can't take credit for it. This is all Naomi."

Esther stopped and stared at him for a moment as if she had never seen him before.

Josias frowned and drew back after placing the casserole dish in the center of the table. "What?"

Esther shook her head slowly, but otherwise didn't answer. "I have rolls and a salad."

"That sounds really good," he said. It'd been ages since he'd had a salad. It was getting to be the perfect weather for it.

"And I have Salisbury steak," Levi said, stepping into the kitchen behind her. Esther moved to one side to allow him entrance.

Levi moved toward the table and set the disposable pan down next to Josias's casserole. Well, Naomi's casserole.

"I know you didn't make that," Levi said with a small chuckle. He pointed toward the casserole dish.

Josias felt heat rising into his cheeks. "Never said that I did."

About that time, Josias's father came into the room, the boys trailing behind him.

Elmer Schrock glanced around, Josias's oldest two boys stuck to his side as if adhered there by glue. Josias could almost see his father's age in that moment, his sadness. First Helen had broken up with Freeman, then she headed off to Lancaster. Returned unwed and pregnant. Now she was gone again, their mother with her, leaving the rest of the Schrocks to fend for themselves. Suddenly he felt for his *mamm*. He had been thinking this whole time about himself and the troubles that her and Helen's leaving had foisted upon him and his life, but of all of them, his mother had the toughest role. She had to either convince Helen to give the baby to another family to raise or force her to stay in New Wilmington. But Josias had no idea what his sister would do if she stayed there. He wouldn't doubt by the time it was all over that Helen would choose to live with Hannah, their older sister, in Dauphin County. As far as he could tell, it was the only solution to a terrible, terrible problem.

Esther stared at the casserole for a moment longer, then flipped her gaze to Levi. "No, he didn't. That's one of Naomi's casseroles."

Josias didn't have anything to say to that. What could he? *Jah*, it was one of Naomi's casseroles. One that he had paid her to make for him, and yet Esther seemed determined to make ripples about the whole situation. It was that fake announcement that she was his fiancée coming back to bite him. It had never been about that truly. He just wanted a nanny, and now the whole thing was getting completely out of hand. Especially when it had his sister glaring at him as if he had taken up with the enemy.

"Speaking of which," Esther said looking around as if expecting someone to jump out from behind the furniture. "Where is Naomi?"

It was a family dinner. Of course, his sister would expect Naomi, as his fiancée, however untrue the rumor, to be there for the family dinner.

"She's with her family tonight." *Because it's her day off.* He sighed. "I told you. We're not engaged."

Esther pressed her lips together and frowned.

"If it tastes half as good as it looks," Levi started, "you should marry her anyway."

"What?" Little ears picked that time to join in the conversation. Dale jumped up and down, looking around at the adults as if he found a golden Easter egg. "You're gonna marry Naomi?"

Josias pressed his lips together and shook his head, needing that physical denial before he could even speak. "No. Now go in the front room, you guys. Go play while we get the rest of dinner on the table."

Dale looked around as if unwilling to leave. Like if he did he might miss something really good.

But Josias was having none of it. "Go on and take your brothers with you."

For a moment Josias thought his son might protest, but then with a reluctant air and heavy feet, he led his younger brothers back into the front room, and Josias could have a little bit of peace while talking to the adults.

"I'm not marrying Naomi," he said, directing the comment toward Esther.

"You broke up?" Her expression became dueling halves of sadness and relief. She had empathy for him, but for some reason she did not want him marrying Naomi Ebersol. But he had no idea why.

"We never broke up," Josias said, then realizing he had totally botched his explanation added, "We were never really engaged."

"But I heard—"

Josias shook his head. "I can't tell you all the particulars, but I came up with the pretend engagement to help Naomi with a problem she has. Then it kind of snowballed on us."

"What kind of problem?" Esther paled, and he knew she was thinking the worst.

He was fairly certain he was going to get vertigo from

shaking his head so much. "No, just stop. Its Naomi's... issue, and I am not at liberty to discuss it."

He had been about to say "problem" but thought better of it. Though he wasn't sure "issue" was any better. But now that the words were out, spoken and floating around between them, there was no taking them back. It was only damage control from here.

"Would somebody please tell me what's going on?" Esther looked close to tears.

Levi glanced back to Josias as if he wanted to tell. Neither man could stand to see their baby sister cry.

Thankfully, Elmer took that moment to step into the conversation. He wrapped Esther into one beefy arm and pulled her close, pressing her head to his shoulder. "Do you remember when the boys were little, and they wouldn't let you play with them? They would climb a tree, and they wouldn't let you go up there with them?"

Esther sniffed and nodded.

"It's kind of like that. Sometimes you just have to let boys play together by themselves and not worry what they're doing when you're not around."

Josias saw Levi puff up just a bit, and for a moment he thought his brother was going to protest at being called a boy, but somehow he managed to keep himself in check and both allowed their father to continue. "Just let them be, Esther," he said. "One day you may understand."

Josias hoped on the same day that Esther got her explanation, he might understand as well.

Chapter Thirteen

Of course, dealing with Esther was a completely different animal than dealing with Dale. Before they even sat down to eat, Josias was in the living room trying to explain to a six-year-old and his younger siblings that, although Naomi would make a wonderful mother and wife, it was all a misunderstanding. Just as Josias had originally told the boys, Naomi was their nanny, and that was all she would ever be. Anybody who said any differently had been hoodwinked.

"So, they're telling lies," Ivan said.

There Josias went shaking his head again. "They're not telling lies. Repeat after me. They have been misinformed."

Ivan nodded as he repeated the words. "Misinformed."

"And it would be best if you didn't say anything to Naomi about this. Do you understand?"

The boys all nodded and promised, and though Josias knew that they would do their best to uphold their oath, he also knew how impulsive and impetuous his children could be. First thing tomorrow morning he needed to head it off with Naomi.

If he had known that it was going to be this complicated when he had stepped in and so chivalrously declared that he and Naomi were getting married, he would have never done it. It felt like he was breaking their hearts over and over again. Even if the heartbreak only lasted for a short time. It seemed to be continual. From having to remind himself that he was not getting married again and that she was too much like Marie, to his boys deciding that she would be a great *mamm* after all. To their families. But it had seemed like a good idea at the time. What was that quote from that English writer? Something about a web of deceit. He wasn't sure what it was, but as far as he could remember, it fit this situation perfectly.

"Let's go get an ice cream," he said first thing on Monday morning.

Naomi stared at him as if he'd grown two heads overnight. "Ice cream?"

Around them the boys cheered, even Tommy who probably didn't quite understand what was going on but couldn't be left out of the fray.

"You know, frozen milk," he said, smiling to take any sting from his words.

"Josias," she started calmly. "It's seven o'clock in the morning. We haven't even had breakfast yet."

As if somehow viewing her as the ultimate voice of reason, the boys all groaned.

"Okay, then," Josias said, switching to a possible Plan B. "We eat breakfast, *then* we go get an ice cream."

Once again she stared at him as if perhaps he had lost his mind. For a split second, he expected her to check him for fever.

"On the off chance, let's say it's eight o'clock by then.

I don't know of any ice cream shops that are open at eight o'clock in the morning."

The boys groaned once more.

"Who said anything about an ice cream shop?" Plan C it was. "We all hop in the buggy, run to the grocery store, buy a couple of cartons of ice cream and then come home and eat it."

Logic won out and cheers rose again from the miniature humans they had surrounding them.

"What has gotten into you?" Naomi asked. She tilted her head to one side as if examining him from a different angle might make things clear.

He loved when she looked at him like that, like he was *ab im kopp*, and yet her smile was filled with l—

No. No, it wasn't filled with any word that began with the letter *L*. That was just his imagination. Something he wanted to see. And something that wasn't fair at all. And he realized in that moment he was truly falling in love with Naomi Ebersol.

"Nothing," Josias said, though his new understanding lent a defensive note to his tone. "I mean, everything's fine. So, ice cream, eight o' clock?"

The boys all cheered.

"I suppose."

That's how you do it, Schrock, he told himself. *Stun them with sheer obstinance.*

He had gotten up early that morning in order to milk the cows that were none too happy to have their schedule even upped by half an hour, but he wanted to stay near the house this morning. Aside from needing to put his ice cream plan into effect, he also wanted to keep the boys from saying anything before he had the chance to talk to Naomi himself.

It was half past eight by the time they had eaten their breakfast, the kitchen was clean, and everyone was washed, changed and in the buggy ready to go to town.

It was an unnecessarily long trip to the Price Chopper grocery store at the end of the valley. When they had church at the bishop's house it was a farther trip than this, but it seemed to take forever. Even with the boys chattering away about what kind of ice cream they were going to vote for when they got to the store and all the other little challenges that come with having five boys crammed into a small space. He felt self-conscious in front of Naomi. This was a new development. He supposed part of it was because last night he had considered that he was falling in love with Naomi, but he had since talked himself out of that idiotic notion. There was no way he could be in love with Naomi. It just wasn't possible. He was never getting married again, for one. Two, if he were to get married again and he were to fall in love—incidentally he was not in love with her, either—it wouldn't be with someone like Naomi Ebersol. It wasn't that she wasn't lovely. She was beautiful and friendly and had the prettiest smile he thought he'd ever seen. It was that faraway look in her eyes that had him putting up his defenses. Though lately that look had become watered-down, almost to the point he couldn't see it anymore, which unnerved him even more.

Yet here the feeling was back again and even stronger.

So maybe he was falling for her…a bit. And that was distorting his view of that look in her eyes, making it where he didn't notice it quite so much. Didn't see how much she was like his Marie, and how she would be unsettled and unhappy for her entire life. It wasn't something he wanted to go through again.

It wasn't that Marie had been nasty or even whiny about the choices she had made. She had simply made them and gone about her life. But he knew. He knew. He could see it in her eyes every time they met. He could feel it in her touch. She knew there was more out there, and until she experienced it, she would never be able to come back and live a quiet life with him. Then again, she might just have run off and never come back. But his Marie had done neither. And she had lived with that suffering every day of her life with him. There was no way he would do that to himself again. No way he could do that to either of them.

When they got to the store, Naomi insisted that they bring all five boys inside with them.

Josias was about to protest when she shook her head and asked him so very sweetly, "Please."

Then she lowered her voice and took a step closer so only he could hear her next words about a newspaper article she had read where a family had been abducted. A family just like this who had left their horse hobbled in the parking lot of a store and gone inside to shop, leaving the kids outside in the carriage all alone. When the parents had come back outside, the carriage, horse and children together were gone. As of the date of the article no one knew where they were.

He was about to tell her that that sort of thing didn't happen in their quiet little valley, but he thought better of it, looking down at that tiny pale hand lying on his arm. The next thing he knew, all seven of them were tromping into the store and over to the freezer section to look at ice cream.

"Is this bubblegum?" Ivan asked, poking one finger against the glass door of the freezer compartment. "It's blue. Is that bubblegum blue?"

Naomi grimaced. "Blue ice cream?"

"You don't know the half of it." He chuckled to himself. *Jah*, Naomi had spent quite a lot of time with her sister's children, but there were two major differences between the Byler girls and the Schrock boys. Age and gender.

"Why don't we get something everybody will like?" Naomi said, circling around the boys to the other side of the freezer cooler.

"Good luck with that," Josias said with a small chuckle. She had no idea what she was in for. From that moment on, a debate ensued. Bubblegum was voted out, as was cotton candy and birthday cake, though vanilla, chocolate and butter pecan were still on the table.

"What's this," Harley asked, pointing at a purple ice cream down on one end.

"That's grape sherbet," Naomi told them.

"Grape?" This sparked the boys' ears up. They all loved grapes. And grape juice. And grape ice pops and pretty much anything that had the flavor.

Naomi must've sensed that weakness and continued to point out flavors. "There's also orange, and lemon, raspberry—it's so good—and lime."

The boys all started hopping up and down, trying to choose their flavor over everyone else. But Naomi held up her hands and shook her head. "Let's do a show of hands. Who wants grape?"

Josias didn't bother to count as she listed off the flavors. She had this under control. In the end it was grape, raspberry and lime.

Naomi gathered up the cartons, and together they headed toward the front.

He leaned a little closer to her, doing his best to ignore the smell of her hair, clean shampoo mixed with sweet baby lotion. "It's a good thing I like sherbet, *jah*?"

She stopped dead still in the grocery store and whirled around to face him. "You do, right?" Her voice was filled with trepidation. And perhaps just a little bit of remorse that maybe she had overstepped her bounds. But he had been just teasing.

"Everybody likes sherbet."

She shook her head at him and started toward the front of the store once more.

"Aren't you guys just the cutest family?"

At the sound of those words, he and Naomi both turned. The boys seemed oblivious to the fact that they had stopped and continued marching toward the front counter. They had taken three more steps when they realized that their *dat* was not behind them.

For a moment Josias was afraid that Naomi was going to say something to the inconsiderate Englisher. He knew they meant well, these people who came to the Amish country and gushed over everything different, including the way the Amish dressed and walked and talked and in general did things as if they were some exhibit at the zoo.

It was obvious the person who had spoken was not from around there. They were definitely a tourist. They did everything but whip out their phone and start taking pictures.

He wrapped one hand around Naomi's arm and gently

tugged her toward the boys, giving the tourists both a nod and a wide berth as they walked away. But Dale was having none of it. He was past them and staring up at the Englisher before Josias blinked a second time.

"We're not a family," Dale said. "She's just helping out for the summer."

"*Jah*," Ivan added. "She's our nanny." His words were emphatic and strong, filled with disbelief at this stranger's audacity. Perhaps Josias had been a little too emphatic when trying to reach his sons and make them understand this relationship he had with Naomi.

The woman looked around at each of them in turn, noting their clothing, their hats, the fact that two of the boys were barefoot, then her gaze fell on Naomi and Josias. Her expression was stunned, and he knew in that moment the woman had no idea what to say.

"I beg your pardon," she finally managed. "It's just that…"

Dale crossed his arms and waited for her to finish. In fact, it seemed several people were waiting for this woman's explanation as to why she assumed that the seven of them made a family just because a man, a woman and a bunch of kids went to the grocery store.

"It's just that," the woman started again, "you make the sweetest looking family I have ever seen. Amish or English. It's obvious you love these boys. And that you care for one another."

Embarrassed and with high color in her cheeks, the woman turned away and scurried down the closest aisle.

She left Josias, the boys and Naomi staring after her.

No one knew what to say. The rest of the onlookers went

back to what they were doing, but to Josias there was no going back.

A family. That was what they had become in the weeks that Naomi had been helping out. They'd eaten practically every meal together, shared birthday cake, and now ice cream.

But that wasn't what truly made up a family.

They all trudged toward the front to pay for their melting sherbet.

The boys were whispering among themselves, but Josias was more concerned about Naomi. She practically hummed with the need to say something, and he had no idea what her reaction was going to be. Was she angry? Indignant? Disbelieving at some people's audacity? Or was she somehow upset with him?

She didn't speak as the cashier bagged their treats and gave Josias his change. Nor did she say anything as they all tromped outside to their waiting buggy. It was only when they had gotten the boys settled and had climbed in themselves that she spoke.

"That was unbelievable." She stared straight ahead, and for a moment he wondered if she was speaking to him at all. But then she turned, and a single tear fell from one eye.

It took everything he had not to wipe it away with his thumb, not to take her into his arms and tell her that it was all going to be okay, whether he knew it to be or not. Firstly, he had no idea why she was crying. Maybe she was one of those people who cried when they got angry. Or maybe she was sad for him because they weren't a family, and they never would be. He had no idea, and he was afraid if he spoke she would fall completely to pieces. She was trembling now, trying to keep it together.

"Some people," he said, keeping his voice as neutral as possible. He'd let her place whatever inflection she wanted on it. Some people were rude. Some people couldn't mind their own business. Some people cared too much. But those words spoken by a stranger only reinforced all that he had been thinking about the night before. How he wished he had not come to her rescue. Then again, he wouldn't have known her. Not like he knew her now. But then he wouldn't be half in love with her, trying to figure out what he was going to do when she left. She would be leaving, there was no doubt about it. The question was, what was he going to do when it happened?

Chapter Fourteen

Naomi was certain her own emotions were going to choke her. And she couldn't even name them all. But the one that stood out the most was regret. That just couldn't be right, though. Regret for what? But she wouldn't let herself think too hard about it as she dished out bowls of sherbet for the boys. One scoop of lime, one scoop of raspberry and one scoop of grape.

"You know when all this melts it's going to be brown and look like chocolate ice cream, right?" Josias said somewhere near her right elbow.

She turned and focused her attention on the top button of his shirt. She hadn't been able to look him in the face since the woman told them they made a wonderful family.

She knew the woman meant well, hadn't meant to break Naomi's heart in two, or bring to light everything in life she wouldn't have.

"I don't think they're going to care," Naomi replied. She turned back to the task at hand, but Josias didn't move away. It was unnerving having him so close and yet she knew he was so far away. He was impossible.

Thankfully, he waited until all the boys were busy eating their sherbet before broaching the subject she knew was inevitable.

"You want to talk about what happened back there?"

She turned from storing the last of the sherbet and gave Josias a tiny shrug. "I don't suppose there's much to really talk about. You know how Englishers can be."

"I do." He nodded.

But she still didn't raise her gaze to his. She felt too raw, too open—as if he could feel every doubt she had.

"But I was talking about in the buggy."

He wanted to know about her tears. He shouldn't be asking. He was her employer. Technically, they weren't even friends, but the past few days, the time she had spent with Josias made her feel like he was a friend. Like she could tell him that the tears were for a family she would never have. And for him. He had told her too many times that he wasn't going to get married again. And she had no cause not to believe him.

She shook her head. "It was nothing. Just overreacting, I suppose." It was as close to the truth that she could get without actually speaking it. She had overreacted.

She felt him study her for a moment, so she quickly grabbed the dishrag and started wiping down the counter. Before long the boys would be back in with empty bowls, and the counter would need to be wiped again, but for now it gave her something to do besides stand there and stare at that tiny little dimple in his chin.

At the table, Tommy patted the tray of his high chair, splattering the melting sherbet from his bowl.

She mentally added mopping the floor—again—to her

list of chores for the day. Just something else to keep her mind off her real problems.

The Englisher today had shown her what she really wanted. Wife, family, husband, children.

But then there was that part of her that yearned for her art. She didn't understand how they both could dwell in her body at the same time. Was it just some joke? She didn't believe that God would tease, but after this summer she was beginning to rethink that possibility.

"I guess I should start looking for a new nanny," Josias said.

"*Jah*," Naomi replied, though even to her own ears, her response sounded doubtful. "So, you're just never going to get married again?" she asked. "Ever? I mean, I don't mean to be nosy or overstep my bounds, but you have a lot to offer a woman. A wife." Her cheeks flamed as she spoke. She could feel the heat coming off her face. But she needed to say those words to him. Because they were true. He did have a lot to offer someone, a new wife, a woman who would take care of him and not be running off to learn how to draw in Philadelphia.

"I can't," he said simply. And yet those words were so complicated.

"Can't," she repeated. Then she turned back and wiped the counter once more. He came behind her, touching her hand and stilling the motion. The warmth of him seeped into her fingers.

But she couldn't stand there like that. She couldn't bask in that touch. She pulled her hand from beneath his and stepped to the side.

"It's just that—" She sensed rather than saw him shake his head. "You didn't know Marie very well."

Great, now he was going to tell her how much he loved his dead wife. And that was right. He should have loved her and should love her still, but Naomi just wasn't sure she was ready to hear about it. She felt too open, too raw.

"I didn't," she managed.

"You would've liked her. Had the two of you gotten to know each other. You are a lot alike."

Naomi didn't know how to respond. Thankfully, Josias continued. "She had dreams, like you. Faraway dreams, but I kept her from that."

"I don't understand," Naomi whispered.

"I'm not really sure myself. But I know that she always felt there was something more out there for her, yet she never had the courage to grasp it. Instead, she married me and had five boys. And then when Annabelle was born—" His voice broke on the last syllable of that name.

Naomi gasped. She had forgotten. How had she forgotten that Josias and Marie had a baby girl who died shortly after she was born? She supposed she was simply too caught up in her own life to give someone else's tragedy much more than a passing thought. She remembered when it happened. She had baked a couple of loaves of bread, a cake and a pie and brought them over for the family. Mattie had brought a casserole and a couple dozen cookies. But after Naomi had done her due diligence and provided something to the grieving family, the implications of it all slipped right past her.

"I'm so sorry," she said, her voice filled with sadness over such a tragedy.

"I thought when Annabelle was born that it would give

Marie something to ground her, but all it did was throw her into a deep depression."

And then she wasted away, or rather that was the consensus in the community. No one really knew for sure, and Naomi wasn't about to ask him such a personal question. Not now. Not yet. Maybe not ever.

"I would never keep you from your dreams, Naomi," he started, his voice quiet and solemn. "But I can't believe that you're going all the way to Philadelphia alone. I've seen you with your family, how much you all care for each other. You joined the church. You'll be excommunicated."

"I'm coming back." But those words weren't as confident as when she had said them before.

"I know that's what you say. But Helen said the same thing. It's just not that easy. And I worry that you—"

"That was good." Dale came into the house, leading the boys all with empty bowls. And just like Josias had said, the mix of flavors had turned brown, making it look like everyone had had chocolate ice cream instead of fruit-flavored sherbet.

But more than that, Naomi knew their conversation was over. He was worried. She was leaving. He wasn't getting remarried. There wasn't much more to say than that.

"Just hang it on the bulletin board," the lady behind the counter at the post office instructed, pointing Josias toward the corkboard suspended on one wall of the foyer. He attached it with pushpins then stood back to look at it.

Nanny wanted. Amish family. Widowed father, five boys.
He had even written the phone number to the phone shanty just down the lane from his house. He had cut in little strips

and written the number vertically so people interested in the position could tear off the number and take it with them. He could hope anyway. He only had a month or so to find someone to take Naomi's place, but he knew that no one could. Not really. Not the way Naomi had insinuated herself into his family.

He and the boys walked out of the post office, each one holding a hand of the other. Josias held Tommy's hand to keep the toddler from running away.

But it was Dale who escaped, letting go of Harley's hand and rushing over to the library. He jumped up and down. "Naomi is in there."

It was only Wednesday, but she had asked for the morning off. For a long break, actually. She came over just at milking time, cooked them breakfast, then left, promising she would be home in time for lunch.

No, not home. Back to his house. Right. She would be back at his little house in order to cook lunch for them today. But he had no idea that she was coming to the library when he had hitched up his own buggy and headed for town.

"Let's go see her!" Ivan said, joining Dale in his excitement. Harley and Eli were close to follow.

Josias swung Tommy up on to his hip. He figured he wasn't getting out of town until they all went in and said hi to Naomi, even though they would see her again shortly.

By the time they got inside, Naomi was no longer standing at the front desk. It didn't take long to find her, seated at one of the computers that lined the far wall.

"Naomi," Dale called.

The librarian shushed him, and he ducked his head apologetically.

But his cry had served its purpose. Naomi turned, a surprised smile on her face as she saw them.

"Hi," she whispered, giving each boy a small hug as they approached.

Tommy kicked to be let down.

Josias set him on his feet, and he ran to Naomi. The sight squeezed Josias's heart. All his sons loved her. And she was leaving. He had a feeling what she was doing on the computer was helping her escape. She had to be looking up her school stuff, preparing to leave. The thought of that made him feel a little queasy.

It was one thing to be married to someone who had a faraway look in their eyes and quite another to know that a person you cared about was leaving and going out into the world alone. Sure, Helen had left, but she had gone to Lancaster with family. Naomi was going to Philadelphia. He had no idea where she was going to live, or how she was going to get around. Did she have a car, did she even know how to drive? She had to have a high school equivalency diploma in order to get into a college, even taking classes that centered around drawing. If she had gone to all that trouble, what else had she done when no one was watching?

"Can we get a book?" Dale asked in a loud whisper, bouncing on his toes.

"Sure," Josias whispered in return.

Ivan pulled on Naomi's arm. "Help us pick out a book," he said in what he considered his inside voice, but most people considered to be two decibels below a yell.

The librarian shushed them again.

Josias bent down closer to his sons. "Remember, we have to whisper."

They all nodded, though he had a feeling they would be shushed several more times before they managed to get out of the library.

"One sec," Naomi said. She turned back to the computer and the buttons on the keyboard then logged off the screen. She stood, pulling the strap of her purse over her shoulder and allowing the boys to grab her arms and tug her toward the children's section.

In no time at all, they had picked out a stack of books and were voting on which one to take home.

They ended up with one about a dragon that ate tacos. It looked utterly ridiculous, but Josias knew his boys liked funny things. They adored the one about food weather, where it rained meatballs, but he hadn't understood one bit of it.

"I hope we're not disturbing you too much," Josias said to Naomi.

She gave him a smile, and as crazy as it sounded, it looked almost sad. "No, I think I was done."

"What's wrong?" He asked the question before he even thought about it. It was none of his business. He shook his head as they walked out of the library, the taco dragon book tucked under Dale's arm. "Never mind. I shouldn't have asked that."

"It's all right," she said.

"If I'd known you were going to come into town today, we could've ridden together, *jah*?"

It was as if a shutter had fallen down on her expression. "*Jah*," she said. But her attitude was anything but open. He didn't quite understand that. However, he had a feeling it had something to do with the Englisher's observation of them as a family. He wasn't sure why. It was just a feeling.

"Is that your buggy there?" Josias asked.

Naomi nodded.

They had parked side by side. Why hadn't he noticed that? Because he hadn't expected Naomi to be in town. He had expected her to be over helping one of her sisters do something, not at the computer visiting the English world.

"I guess I'll see you at the house then," Josias said.

Naomi swung up into her buggy and gave him a quick nod. In a flash she pulled out and was headed down the road, Josias staring after her, still wondering what was wrong.

"Will you read us the book tonight before bed?" Harley asked as they settled around the table to eat supper.

After they had gotten back from town, Naomi had done her best to hide her worry. But Josias must have been able to sense it. He asked her twice what the matter was, but she wasn't ready to talk about it. Wasn't sure how to even say the words.

"I'll be at my house when it's time for you to go to bed," she told him gently. She left after the supper dishes were washed and put away. Hours before bedtime.

"You can spend the night," Eli said helpfully. Or maybe not so helpfully.

"I'm not sure that would be the best thing to do." That was putting it mildly. They were already under watch since they were "engaged," and she was working at his home. Spending the night was completely out of the question.

Josias cleared his throat, but as had been her trend this week, she couldn't look him in the eye.

"Why not?" Dale asked. "Buddy at school has sleepovers all the time."

"*Jah*. I'm sure he does, but with grown-ups it's a little different."

"Why?" Ivan asked.

"*Jah*, why?" Harley echoed.

Josias coughed.

Naomi turned to him for help, and for the first time since their "almost kiss" she looked at him. Really looked at him. Handsome, godly, a little bit tired and quite a bit panicked.

"It's just one of those things," Naomi said, hoping it would stick as a satisfactory answer.

"But Dawdi and Mammi spend the night together. Why can they, and you can't? They are adults, too." Dale was really on a roll tonight.

Easy enough. "Because they are married. Married couples get to have sleepovers for the rest of their lives."

"Then you and Dat should get married," Dale announced, and the sentiment was echoed by all his siblings.

Josias coughed again. Choked, really. Naomi turned her attention to him.

Help me! she mouthed.

Josias cleared his throat once more. "Hang on. Hang on," he said, doing his best to calm them down. "That is a nice thought, but there's a little more to marriage than you boys...understand."

"Tell us, tell us, tell us," Harley chanted.

It was Josias's turn to look to her for assistance.

"There's love," she said simply.

"You don't love my *dat*?" Dale asked.

The other boys waited with rapt attention for her answer.

"Of course I do." She almost choked herself when she said the words. "But it's not like that."

Except it was.

She had gone and fallen for Josias Schrock and his rowdy little family. She adored them all. But Josias had already told her that he would never get married again. And she was going away to school. There wasn't a path that they could share.

Once again their gazes snagged, and Naomi found that she couldn't look away. Something had changed. Something had shifted between them, and she had no idea what it was. Yet she could see the alteration on Josias's face, in his soft gray eyes.

She would have to wait until supper was finished and the dishes washed and put away before she could ask him what it was. But by the time they got there, her heart was pounding in her chest, and her hands were shaking.

"I'll walk you out," Josias said, stopping the boys who had it in mind to follow them out to her buggy. "You stay here," he told them.

For a moment she thought they might protest, but they were good boys, obedient, and they did as their father instructed.

And that made it worse. Now she was all alone with Josias. The kids were probably all watching from the window. Not that there would be anything really to see. It wasn't like he was going to kiss her.

He wasn't. He wouldn't. At least she didn't think that he would. Not with the children watching. And they weren't really engaged. Not that kissing would be allowed then, either. Such activities were exclusive to married couples.

Which was exactly what she thought he was going to talk to her about. She had stewed on the situation all through supper, trying to figure out what had changed. The only thing she could think of was her feelings for him. She had realized that she loved him, and the truth must have been shining on her face for him to see. She loved him, and he knew. He was probably going to tell her that he would make do until he found someone to help him with the boys. That she was relieved of her duties.

He didn't say a word as he left her side to go to the paddock and retrieve her horse. He brought the beast back over to the carriage where she waited, uncomfortable in the silence and her own thoughts.

If he did fire her, it would spell disaster for her on so many levels. After checking her email today and seeing just how much school was really going to cost her, her dream was beginning to look hopeless. She had been saving for a long time now, but what she had thought had been a straightforward price was not. There were other fees and living expenses and books and materials and all sorts of other things they were now telling her that she needed. And if it was changing now, she wasn't sure it wouldn't change again in the future.

It seemed like her dream was slipping away right before her eyes. What really confused her was the fact that she wasn't entirely sad to see it go. It was something of a relief. As if she had built it up in her mind too high to ever be realized. If that were the case, she was better off staying right where she was.

But was it the case?

Or was it merely time to dig in and fight for what she wanted?

Josias finished hitching up her horse and returned to her side.

No more time. No more reprieve. Whatever was on his mind, now was the time for him to say it.

"Nice night," he murmured.

Maybe he was as nervous about broaching the subject as she. But why? It wouldn't change his life that much to fire her. She was certain he could find someone to take her place. The thought made her stomach lurch, but it was the truth. She loved him, but he had already explained that she was a little too much of a dreamer to suit his future needs. And he was never getting married anyway.

"Just say it, Josias," she cried. "Whatever it is, just tell me."

He blinked as if shocked, maybe even confused by her outburst. "Okay," he said slowly, then looked as if he were gathering courage. He ran his hands down the front of his pants and cleared his throat. "Marry me."

Chapter Fifteen

As far as marriage proposals go, Josias figured his was at the bottom of how to do it. But he walked out here, running the words over in his mind again and again, feeding his resolve and formulating his argument on why the two of them should marry. And just when it got to the point where he felt like he could say the words, she demanded he tell her. Now she looked as shocked as if he had poked her with a cattle prod.

"Marry you?" Naomi stared back at him. They were surrounded by night. Darkness, stars, the sound of insects calling to one another. It was the perfect June night. And he had gone and messed it up.

"*Jah*," he said. He had surprised himself by coming up with this idea, surprised himself even further by carrying it through. Now it looked like he was in for a battle. "The boys love you. That's apparent. And I don't know what happened today with your school, but I could tell it was something bad. I know that's your dream, but we can make a good life together."

"I don't have enough money to go to school," she admitted.

He figured it was something along those lines. "Just

think about it," he said, bringing the conversation around to a topic he was less comfortable with but needed to be addressed. "You don't have to answer today. And if you don't get the money, well, like I said, we can make a good life together."

It was not the best argument, but the only one he could come up with at the time. Since she had come to be his nanny and they had gotten to know each other, it seemed like there were a thousand reasons why the two of them could be a couple, excluding the fact that she was too much like Marie and too much of a dreamer, but that didn't mean she couldn't be happy there. Marie was happy until Annabelle died.

"Please, just promise me you'll think about it," he begged.

She nodded and swallowed hard. But he couldn't read what was going on in those ocean-colored eyes. He supposed his proposal on top of discovering that she might not be able to go to school anyway was a bit much. Perhaps he should've waited. What was done was done, though. And he would just have to ride it through.

He backed up a step. He wanted to give her space to make her decision, but more than that he needed to have her out of arm's reach. Because he so badly wanted to grab hold of her and pull her close and kiss her and promise her that he would make her life better than anything else she could dream of. Even if he knew those words might not be true. Perhaps that was why. Because he knew they weren't true. He could only give her what he could give her, and she would have to decide its value for herself. He couldn't force that. No matter how badly he wanted to.

She backed up as well, as if reluctant to turn away. Finally, she did so and climbed into her buggy and set the horse into motion. Josias stood watching her as she drove away, surprised by his own actions, but knowing still that it was the right thing to do.

Naomi pulled in front of her house and stopped the horse, surprised to realize she couldn't remember most of the drive home. Her thoughts had been going in circles, chasing each other around trying to figure out where she fit into everything that happened today.

Her dream of art school seemed to be at an end. And the more time she spent with Josias, the less appealing going away to Philadelphia became.

Then tonight he asked her to marry him. After telling her that he was never getting married again. What had changed? She had seen it on his face at supper—that shift, that dawning of a new plan, a new idea, a new path. Yet she didn't understand where it had come from. They were talking about sleepovers and bedtime stories. It just didn't fit.

Yet something had shifted. When he realized that he needed someone full-time for his boys? Was that all this was to him?

She swung down from the buggy and went about putting the horse away for the night, her thoughts still churning as she brushed down the mare.

In all that he said after his proposal, he never once mentioned love for her. It wasn't unusual to have marriages that didn't revolve around romantic love. Especially not second marriages like it would be for him. Love could grow between two people, especially when those two people were already married and knew that emotion needed to be nurtured to make the family whole. This wasn't her second marriage, and she loved him so much. So much so it almost took her breath away.

She was even more breathless from storing the carriage by the time she climbed the steps and made her way through the front door. It wasn't late, but the house was quiet.

Her *dat* was in the living room reading the paper. He loved reading the contributors' stories in the back of *Die Botschaft*, where Amish men and women from all around the country sent in updates as to their farms, community happenings and just life in general.

"Where is everybody?" If it'd been a Thursday she would've thought everyone was at the youth group meeting. But it wasn't Thursday. It was Wednesday.

"Naomi." Her *dat* folded up the paper, even as he stared at her over his reading glasses. "I didn't hear you come in."

That was because she was too involved in her own thoughts to make any noise at all, she supposed. "Sorry," she said. What was she sorry for? Not disturbing her *dat*? Josias's proposal was making her a little wonky.

Her father recognized it as well, tilting his head to one side and studying her. "Everything okay?"

Naomi made her way into the living room and sat on the couch. Perched there really, as if someone was about to poke her and make her jump up once more. That was how she felt, antsy, prickly, like a stranger in her own skin. Like she didn't belong anywhere, not even in her own body.

Lord, please help me through this. There's an answer. There's a solution. Please show me the way. Amen.

"*Jah*," she said, though they both knew it wasn't the truth. "So where is everybody?"

"Evie is out with Freeman somewhere, and Lizzie and Sarah Ann went over to help Esther Schrock with something or another. I think a dress." He shook his head as if the ways of women were beyond him. "Priscilla's upstairs with the twins."

Of all her sisters, Priscilla was perhaps the least likely for her to get the best answer from. Or so she thought. Maybe discussing this with Priscilla was the right thing to do. She would definitely give Naomi a new perspective.

"Are you going to tell me what happened?" Dat asked. "Or are you just going to let me sit here and worry?"

She shook her head. "There's nothing for you to worry about." There was nothing wrong with her. She wasn't sick or hurt. She had just been asked to marry a man whom she loved who did not love her in return.

"You know you can talk to me about anything, right?" His words were solemn and held the weight of the world. *Jah*, she knew she could talk to her father about almost anything. But she wasn't quite ready to tell him that she had dreams of going to art school, and she certainly wasn't ready to tell him she had a marriage proposal from Josias Schrock. Some things needed to be thought about a little bit longer.

"I know that, Dat," she said, twisting her fingers in the edge of her apron. Honestly, she didn't want to talk to anybody about either subject right now. She wanted to go upstairs and draw, put her thoughts on paper through art. It was the way she had always been. Maybe in drawing something, anything, she could get these stampeding thoughts in some sort of order.

"So, when were you going to tell me about art school?"

His words fell unceremoniously between them. And still they took her breath away.

"How—how do you know about that?" She didn't have to ask really, she knew who let that cat out of the bag. One of her sisters, for certain. Most likely—

"Priscilla," he said, echoing her own thoughts. Leave it to her twin to tell all. It was like being three again.

"I don't know," Naomi started, shaking her head as she spoke. "I don't think it's going to happen anyway. She should have never said anything." Anger rose up in her like heat off the asphalt in August. She stood.

"I'm glad she did. I would've never known otherwise."

And that was why she hadn't told him yet. It was up to her to say, not her twin. "You would have. I would've told you eventually." She would've had to. She wasn't going to just disappear for four years without telling her father where she was going. "Besides, I just found out today that I don't have enough money to go." And she didn't think she could take out any kind of loan for this. That just seemed frivolous, somehow. Saving her money to go was one thing, but borrowing money to live out the dream that she would eventually have no use for in her life was not something she could stomach.

"Sit down, Naomi," her father said, finally putting the paper aside.

She did as he bade. She was a good Amish girl after all.

Her father pushed his reading glasses to the top of his head, perching them in the center of the growing bald spot there. "That's why I wish you would've come to me first."

"I don't understand, Dat," she said, her voice a little impatient. But it had been something of a day. And she was ready to go upstairs and crawl under the covers. Perhaps cry a bit, draw some and try to figure out if she could be in a loveless marriage with Josias Schrock. Well, it wouldn't be loveless on her part. How would she get through something like that?

Her father picked up an envelope lying next to him on the table that also held his reading lamp. "I'm not sure how much money you need, but here is the first installment. We'll figure out the rest after that."

Naomi's world tilted on its head. "What?" She must be losing it. All the stress and worry were getting to her. She thought her father was trying to give her money to go away in the English world to art school. But that just couldn't be happening.

Her father nodded patiently and gestured once more with the envelope he held, urging her to take it from him. "If art school is what you want, art school is what you will have."

She took the envelope from him, her fingers trembling. She lifted the flap to see a stack of one-hundred-dollar bills, probably as much, if not more than she had saved in that shoebox under her bed. "I—I don't know what to say," she whispered in awe. How was this happening?

"*Danki* will do for starters." Her father smiled.

"*Danki*," she automatically whispered. But she needed to say more. Much, much more. Though like her churning thoughts, those words were whirling around in her head, mixed up with everything else. She had settled herself on not going to art school on the drive home from Josias's house. That dream seemed so far away, unreachable. Unattainable. So, the question had become could she marry Josias knowing he didn't love her? Or could she stand not being married to him, loving him, and watch him get remarried to someone else? Because she could only imagine that the shift she'd seen in him had been about the care of his boys. No, he wouldn't get married for himself. But he would do it for his children. Could she stand by and watch that happen?

Now art school was back. She held her dream in her hands. She was torn.

"I can't accept this," she said, offering the money back to him.

He shook his head and refused to take the envelope from her. Instead, he took something from beside his chair, tucked away where she hadn't been able to see it. It was a portfolio-type envelope, the kind that held large papers and was closed by a little string that wound around a fastener.

"Look here." He pushed the portfolio toward her.

She was so numb that she dropped the envelope into her lap and accepted the portfolio that he gave her.

But she sat there a heartbeat and just stared at it.

"Go ahead." Her father nodded toward her. "Open it."

After all the surprises that had been thrown her way this day, Naomi was a little reluctant to go digging in something that wasn't hers, but her father seemed urgent in his need for her to see what was inside.

She unwound the little string, fingers shaking so badly she dropped it twice and had to start over.

Her father waited. He had the patience of Job. She knew no man except for perhaps Josias who was so understanding, patient and caring about every little thing.

Finally, she got the portfolio open and pulled the loose

papers from inside. What met her eyes was surprising, to say the least.

Drawings. Paper upon paper of drawings she had never seen. They weren't hers, so…

"Whose are these?" she asked, barely glancing up at her father as she said the words. The drawings were beautiful, and some she recognized as her and her sisters when they were younger. There was one of her father with a full head of hair and another of the puppy they had when she was a child. They were breathtaking, gorgeous. Not exactly real life but a muted representation, which gave them an almost dreamlike quality. The mere sight of them made her stomach hurt with longing. Then she got to the last one. It was a picture of her mother.

Tears welled in her eyes. Her mother had been gone long enough that memories of her were starting to fade. Naomi could no longer remember the sound of her mother's voice. And her face was starting to merge with that of her sisters. She wondered if she would ever be able to visualize her mother again. And here she was on paper, staring back at her, beautiful blond hair, gorgeous green eyes. Bright and healthy before the cancer had struck her down.

"That's how she wanted to be remembered," her father said. His words were thick with emotion, clogged with tears. Naomi blotted her own with the back of one sleeve. She couldn't let them fall on the artwork she held. It was simply too precious.

"I know I should've shown you these a long time ago but…" He shook his head. "I just couldn't bear to look at them myself."

"Did you…?"

Her father shook his head. "No, art was your mother's love. Second to you girls of course."

"Where did she—"

Apparently, Naomi was destined to not be able to finish any of her sentences tonight.

"It was a God-given talent."

A God-given talent that had to be hidden. A bright light under a bushel. That didn't seem quite right, and yet it was the way it was.

"If she knew you could draw like you do, she would be so proud to know that she handed that down to you."

So, she had inherited more than that bit of green in her eyes and her blond hair from her mother. She had received a love of pictures.

"That's why I tell you not to worry about art school. We'll find a way. If that's what you want to do then you shall have it, Naomi."

She bit back a sob, overcome with choices and blessings and love and grief and regret and everything else the day had brought to her. Then she took a steadying breath. She had to keep it together. For herself. For her father. He had shown her something unbelievably precious, and she needed to see it through before she let go of her emotions.

She slid the pictures back into the portfolio and somehow managed to wind the little string around the disk that held it all in place. Then reluctantly, she handed it back to her father. She wanted to keep it, look at the pictures some more.

"*Danki*, Dat," she said, straightening her spine and swallowing back the overwhelming feelings of love and regret for all the people in her life. "I know this is going to sound strange," she said, "after what Priscilla told you, but can I have a little time to think this over?"

His eyebrows crinkled and crashed together above his caring blue eyes. "Of course," he said, but his expression was one of confusion mixed with just a smidge of hurt. That was not her intention. But she couldn't help it. This was something that had to be thought through. Even if she couldn't tell him that the one thing that might keep her from going to art school was marrying Josias Schrock.

"Hi."

Well, that wasn't awkward at all. For the first time in his life, Josias wished he had pockets in his pants. He would love to shove his hands inside them so he would have something to do with them. Instead, they just flopped at his sides as he watched Naomi walk into his house on Thursday.

She stopped just inside the door. He had to admit, she looked beautiful today. Even with the dark circles under her eyes. She still had a touch of color to her cheeks, from excitement or embarrassment, he had no idea. Either way, it looked good on her.

"Hi." She set her purse down on the pie safe and approached. "Where are the boys?"

"Still upstairs, though once they figure out you're here, they'll be down." And that would leave them no time at all to talk about last night. There was this part of him that wanted to take back that proposal. To not confuse her with choices other than going to art school. But if she wasn't getting the money, maybe he stood a chance. But did he really want to be a second choice?

As if on cue, thundering footsteps could be heard echoing down the stairwell. A few seconds later, the boys burst into the room, Tommy toddling behind. His bright red hair stood up all around, and someone had helped him into his clothes. His shirt was half out of his pants and half in but at least his suspenders were straight.

"You're here." Harley wrapped his arms around her and hugged her as if he never wanted to let her go. As if she wasn't coming back. But if she went away to art school she wouldn't be coming back, and she would disappear just like their mother had. He knew Harley couldn't remember his *mamm*, but Josias knew the boy still suffered a loss that had nothing to do with memories.

"I told you I would be," she said. "All summer long." When she said the words, she didn't look anywhere near Josias. Not that he expected her to, but to him it seemed like she was doing her best not to look at him at all. And that was when he knew something had happened. That was when he knew she wasn't going to marry him.

Naomi had wanted to talk to Josias first thing in the morning. She was still going to work the summer for him as she had promised, but at the same time... It was going to be awkward. But what choice did she have? She stayed awake most of the night tossing and turning over the choices that had been offered her that day. She was so impossibly torn between the two. The woman in her wanted to marry the man she loved, to raise his little family. Maybe even have some children of her own, God willing, and live out all her days in Millers Creek. The daughter in her felt some sort of obligation to carry through with a dream that was not really hers exclusively, but that belonged to her mother as well.

The picture of her mother was burned into her brain. It was how her mother wanted to be remembered. Perhaps that was why Naomi wanted to draw, to remember things, so that others could remember things, but still art could be vanity and that was frowned upon. If she wanted to carry out this mission of remembrance, she would have to leave the Amish and stay gone.

The thought made her feel queasy, like the time she got into a fishing boat with her *dat* and he rocked it from side to side.

Yet there was this sense of obligation that she had never felt before. She had her mother's talent and her father's money. There was no other choice, and yet the thought made her want to cry. But could she really stay and get married to a man who did not love her? Who just wanted her to be a nanny for his children? Who was willing to go back on his own vow to never get married again so that he could have that?

The boys had gone outside to play for the afternoon while Naomi did the lunch dishes and started mending shirts. For some reason their elbows always tended to get ripped on something. But that was boys, right?

"Are you alone?"

She closed her eyes just briefly. She set her sewing in her lap and looked up to Josias. She smiled, hoping the curve of her lips looked sincere enough to pass. She didn't feel like smiling. "For the time being." But who knew when something would erupt outside that they would bring into the house for her to settle?

Josias came into the living room and eased down into the chair opposite her. She had placed her sewing basket on the couch next to her so that spot was taken, and truly she was glad to have the coffee table between them.

"Josias—"

He shook his head. "You don't have to answer. I—I can see what your answer is."

He could see? She barely knew her own mind, yet he could tell that she was going to turn down his proposal?

"Honestly, I should've never asked you to marry me."

Those words were like a knife in her heart, and she couldn't control her sharp intake of breath, as the pain seared through her.

"It wasn't fair of me," he continued. "I know you'll have a great time in Philadelphia." He pushed to his feet, and Naomi ducked her head to hide the threatening tears. "I just hope you'll stay with me until the end of the summer. At least until I can find someone."

Naomi couldn't lift her head. Couldn't look at him lest she burst into tears. Lack of sleep and overwhelming emotions were eating her up inside. One look at his handsome face, and she knew she was going to lose it. She needed time to collect herself before truly facing him once more. Hastily, she set the shirt aside, barely securing the needle before she pushed to her feet. "Excuse me," she said and rushed from the room.

If Josias thought her exit was strange, he at least didn't come after her. Perhaps because she ran into the bathroom and shut and locked the door. She couldn't look at herself in the mirror. She didn't want to see herself, didn't want to see the desperation and sadness reflected there. Even if she wanted to marry him, and truly she did, she wished he'd never proposed to her. Those words hurt most of all.

* * *

As far as he could tell, Naomi was going out of her way to avoid him. Now he had gone and done it. He had made things awkward between them. When she told him that she couldn't afford school, he shouldn't have offered her marriage, he should've offered her more money. Money to live out her dream.

It was something he didn't understand, this dream to go away. He was tethered to this land. His first wife was buried here, his daughter was buried here, he would be buried here. And perhaps Naomi would return someday happy to settle down. And who knew? Perhaps by then, he would be in the market to marry once more. But until that time, he had to find another solution.

He pulled his buggy to a stop in front of his *dat*'s house, anxious to see if there had been any word from Helen and his *mamm*. Not that he really expected any. He had to get out of the house. He had to get away from Naomi. So, he had left his boys in her care and made the short trip to see his brother. He wasn't sure what Levi could offer him other than conversation and distraction, but right now he'd take what he could get.

"Hey! What are you doing here?" His brother came out onto the porch to greet him.

Josias set the brake on the buggy and looped the horse's reins around the hitching post before facing his brother. "I just had to get out of the house."

Levi gave him a strange look. "Why?"

Josias glanced at the ground at his feet. "No reason," he said even though it was not the truth. But did he really want to tell his brother all the reasons that drove him here today?

"Come on in here." Levi motioned with one arm for Josias to come in the house.

"Where's *Dat*?"

"Down in one of the fields with Esther."

"What are you doing up here then?"

Levi lifted his left hand, a bloodied rag wrapped around it. "I cut myself."

"That looks bad," Josias said.

"Nah," Levi said. "It'll be okay in a minute. I'm just about to put a bandage on it." He gestured toward the table, where gauze and medical tape waited.

Josias eased down into the opposite seat and waited for Levi to take his own chair. "Are you sure that doesn't need stitches?"

Levi chuckled. "No. I'm not a doctor. But I got these fancy little things here are supposed to keep it shut. I figure if I can keep the skin together for a little bit it will grow back and be fine."

That was his brother. So much like his *dat*. More old-fashioned than anything else. Not in a bad way. Just in that way of those who came before them. A person didn't go to a doctor unless they were practically dying, and they didn't mingle with Englishers, and they sure didn't run off to art school in Philadelphia.

"I heard something the other day," Levi said, as he started placing bandages carefully over his wounded finger.

"Oh *jah*? What was that?"

Levi kept his attention trained on the task at hand even as he spoke. "I heard that Naomi Ebersol is going to some fancy art school in Philadelphia."

Josias felt his mouth go dry. Somehow he managed to swallow and reply, "Really? Who told you that?"

"Esther. Seems Evie told her. And it's getting all around town."

Josias was sure it was. That was just how things went in their little community. But he supposed that everyone was going to find out sooner or later.

"I told you the engagement was just gossip."

"*Jah*, you did. But I saw the way you two looked at each other when you didn't think anyone was looking at you."

It took Josias a moment to make those words make sense, but when they did, he shook his head. "I don't look at Naomi any way and she doesn't look at me any way and I don't know what you're talking about."

"You're telling me you're not in love with her, is that it?" His brother never lifted his gaze.

"It doesn't matter if I am," Josias said.

Levi completed his task and held his finger up to admire his handiwork. He turned his hand this way and that. Then dropped it to the table and pinned Josias with his hard amber gaze. "Why is that?"

"I asked her to marry me last night," Josias admitted. "And today she turned me down." How it hurt to say those words, but he supposed he should get used to them. Not only were people going to wonder about Naomi going away to art school, they were going to wonder what was wrong with Josias that she broke up with him. If only he could get the rumor of the fake engagement grounded before the rumor of her going to art school made the rounds. But it seemed that wasn't going to happen. Not if Levi was already in the know about Naomi's plans.

"She said that. She told you 'no' straight out."

"She didn't have to," Josias said, the words even more painful than the rest of this conversation had been. "She didn't have to because I can see it on her face. She's too much like Marie. I should've never—"

"She's nothing like Marie," Levi said with a frown. "Why would you say that?"

"Because Marie—she was always dreaming about something bigger than what she had here. I know if she hadn't married me, she would've left. Then I thought when Annabelle was born—" Josias couldn't finish. He didn't need to—Levi knew the story.

"Annabelle was born and died, and Marie wasted away until she died as well. She might've wanted bigger and better things, but she never went for them. She didn't have that much bravery. Not like Naomi has."

He couldn't argue with that. Every word was true. Naomi was brave and strong, strong enough to go out in the English world and survive just fine. Even if she never returned. And there was nothing he could do about that. Nor was there anything he wanted to. More than anything he wanted Naomi to be happy. And if art school was going to make her happy, then that was what he wished for her, even if it broke his heart.

"So, you're telling me you don't love her?"

Josias had been too involved in his own thoughts. "Huh? Who? Marie?"

Levi shook his head. "Naomi. You're telling me you don't love Naomi Ebersol."

Josias shook his head. "I do love her," he said. "I told

you that. I love her enough that I proposed to her last night, and she turned me down."

"But she didn't tell you no," Levi said. "Or did she?"

She hadn't. Josias hadn't given her the opportunity to. He didn't want to hear those words come out of her mouth. He didn't want the finality of her answer. It was one thing to know and another thing to hear it.

"Perhaps she should have given you the answer," Levi said.

"Why?" Josias said.

"I told you, I've seen of the two of you look at each other. And she loves you."

If only it were true. "What do you know about love?" Josias asked.

Levi's amber eyes darkened. "You'd be surprised."

By the time church rolled around, Naomi was about to burst. Too many things had happened, too much had gone on. Now everyone in the community knew that she was going to art school. She wasn't sure how the rumor got around, but it was going around. Perhaps Josias had said it. The thought made her angry. But she just couldn't wrap her mind around him spreading that sort of gossip. True or not. And for some reason now that the news was out in the world, it felt more like an obligation than ever before.

What truly bothered her though most of all was that she felt certain that everyone believed that she had dumped Josias in order to run off to art school. No matter how many times she claimed that they were never engaged…it seemed happy news no matter how fake was hard to squash. People wanted an engagement, a marriage. They wanted to believe in love. They didn't want to believe that she would leave their sweet community behind and go off to the big city and live among the English.

Her father hadn't stopped smiling since he had handed her that envelope of money, though she sometimes caught a splash of sadness in his eyes even through that smile. He was proud of himself for what he had done. He had carried on his wife's talent through her. Even if that talent was *verboten*. And Naomi was more confused than ever.

She prayed and prayed and prayed some more. But when no answer came to her, she did the only thing she knew to do. She baked.

She spent all of Saturday baking: cakes, pies, muffins, cornbread, even scones. Up until that point, she had no idea what a scone was. But she had made them. Maybe she would spend the afternoon taking them to folks, but she didn't want to. She didn't want to see their looks, she didn't want to answer their questions, and she sure didn't want to defend a decision she truly hadn't made to go to art school.

But it didn't matter, Josias didn't want to marry her. If she was going to be an old maid, she might as well be an old maid who did some things in life that she enjoyed.

Somehow she made it through Sunday, though she did hitch a ride with Mattie and Samuel so she could go home early. She wasn't sure how she was going to get home, but she figured she would spend the night and have one of them run her over to Josias's in the morning for work. From there, maybe he would take her home. Or she could get her *dat* to come fetch her. Either way, she just had to get out of there before one more person gave her *that look*.

"I just don't understand it," Mattie said, bouncing baby Davida on her shoulder as she rubbed her back to burp the infant. Davida had proven to be something of a challenge, deciding that she preferred a bottle with formula to her mother's milk. Naomi knew that Mattie was heartbroken over the baby's choice, but the girl had to eat, so she was fed what she preferred, even if the *mamm* shed a few tears over it. "He asked you to marry him, and then he told you he wished he hadn't. Correct?"

Thankfully Samuel was outside with the girls. Naomi figured he did it just so she and Mattie could have a moment of privacy. For that she was thankful.

"It doesn't matter," Naomi said. "Mattie, if you could've seen Dat when he showed me that picture."

She had wanted everyone to get together and look at those pictures, but she hadn't managed to find the courage to have her *dat* bring them out once more. There was something so utterly personal about them that it made her want to keep the memories secure even if she never saw them again. And perhaps she might not ever see them again. Her father had waited this long to show them to her.

"I hope I get to see them," Mattie said. "Sometimes I can't picture her face."

Her sister didn't need to tell Naomi how sad it was to have that happen. She had experienced it herself as well.

"He was so proud of himself to give me that money. Even if Josias came in here right now and offered to marry me again, I couldn't accept."

Mattie stopped bouncing and patting Davida to stare open-mouthed at Naomi.

"What?" Naomi said.

"But you love him."

To hear her sister say it seemed so simple, yet it was anything but. "It doesn't matter."

"Love is all that matters. Jesus taught us that."

But the greatest of these is love.

"It doesn't matter because he doesn't love me."

"How do you know that?"

Naomi flopped down on the sofa and sighed. "All the time he was telling me about how good of a marriage we would have together, he never once mentioned love. He said the boys loved me and we can build a good life. But he never said *he* loved me."

"Men are clueless," Mattie said. "I mean, they can fix fences and take care of the animals and grow crops and a hundred other things. But when it comes to love, men have no idea. Don't you think that when he told you that the two of you could have a good life together that he was telling you that he loves you?"

"No, I don't think so."

"I do know this," Mattie said. "Even if you're not going to marry Josias, don't go to art school just because Dat said he would pay. Don't go to art school because of Mamm. You go to art school because it's what you want to do."

Those words echoed and reverberated around Naomi for the rest of the evening. Even when she went into the spare bedroom to sleep, she didn't sleep. She just kept hearing them over and over. *You go to art school because it's what you want to do.* Followed by, *Don't you think that when he told you that the two of you could have a good life together that he was telling you that he loves you?*

Was that it? Had he been telling her that he loved her, and she was just too wrapped up in everything else to hear what he was saying? She just didn't know. There was only one way to find out.

She would go tomorrow and ask him.

Lord, please help me, guide my footsteps. Help me accept what Josias says. Help me tell him how I feel about him. You tell us love is the greatest we can have. Please, God, help me find it. Aemen.

She was dead on her feet when she got up Monday morning. But she got up with a new determination.

Thankfully she had a few dresses still left at Mattie's from when she stayed after David died, and she put on one of those to go to work as Josias's nanny. By the end of the day, she wondered if that would still be her title. Was she really going to look him in the face and have him tell her that he didn't love her?

She loved her sister. And she trusted her. Mattie was smart and savvy. But she was human and could be wrong. It was a big chance Naomi was taking. But if she didn't take it...

If she didn't take it, she would regret it for the rest of her life. She might not go to art school. She had the rest of the summer to figure that out. But one thing was certain, if Josias loved her and wanted to marry her, well, art school paled by comparison.

Samuel was the one to drive Naomi to Josias's house that morning. She had no idea how much Mattie had told her husband about the situation, but every now and then Naomi could feel Samuel's gaze land on her then flick away like a scared fly. It, along with the clip-clop of the horse's hooves and the whir of the iron-rimmed wheels on the asphalt, was about to make her scream. Normally, those sounds were soothing, but today they were off beat with her pounding heart. And it just made her feel like the world was closing in.

And maybe it was. Maybe she would get there, and Josias would tell her that Mattie was wrong. That he cared for her as a person, but he didn't love her like a wife. What would she do then?

She would decide that after. Right now, she just needed to know the truth.

Her hands were sweaty as Samuel pulled his buggy to a stop in front of Josias's house. "Do you want me to go in?"

Naomi shook her head, probably a little too vigorously. Then she stopped. "No. I'm fine. Tell Mattie thanks."

"She told me to tell you good luck."

"Thanks," she said as she climbed down from the buggy and made her way up the porch steps, into the house and—

Pandemonium. She was pretty sure that was the word. Pandemonium reigned. The best she could figure, someone had decided to cook breakfast without waiting for her. Pots bubbled on the stove, and pancake batter dripped down the front of the oven from the griddle on top. Milk, eggshells and flour were strewn about. The smell of burnt bacon hung in the air like a cloud.

And the boys. Dale and Ivan were arguing over the spatula, each one with a hand on its handle. Each was jerking it toward himself, obviously fighting for control.

She took a quick step back as a kitten ran across her feet, Tommy close behind, squealing as he ran, fingers outstretched to grab the poor beast. Harley was sitting in the middle of the floor, head thrown back and sobbing wildly.

Eli and Josias were nowhere to be seen. She took all that in in a split second, then jumped into action.

She pulled the boiling pot off the stove, careful not to drip it on Tommy as he raced by, chasing the cat once again. Into the sink it went, oatmeal and all. Apparently bacon wasn't the only burnt smell floating in the air.

She grabbed another spatula and flipped the pancake only to realize it was a little too late. So, she scooped it up once again and put it in the trash. With things on the stove under control, she turned back to the boys. She walked over to Dale and Ivan and didn't say a word. She merely outstretched her hand for them to hand over the cooking utensil. They did so without question.

"You two sit down on the couch and think about what it means to be brothers," she told them. Each one crossed their arms and marched into the living room to do as she bade.

She was on her way to see about Harley when the cat raced by. She deftly scooped it into her arms. Tommy stopped next to her, jumping up and down and squealing, "Ditty. Ditty. Ditty."

"No, Tommy, you may not terrorize the kitty," she told him. "Go sit down with your brothers." When he didn't immediately obey, she called the two boys back into the room. They were still pouting slightly, but they did as she asked.

"Ivan, take Tommy into the living room and you guys work a puzzle for a while." Then she turned to Dale. "Please take this cat outside and put him back in the barn where he belongs."

"That one is a girl," he told her.

Fine, then. "Put *her* in the barn where *she* belongs."

Dale nodded. "Yes, Mamm."

Her heart squeezed at the term. He probably didn't even realize he said it. But it meant so much to her. Yes, she wanted to be a *mamm* to these kids. And even more than that, she wanted to be a wife to Josias. But there was one very important question she needed to ask him before it could become reality.

She bent down and scooped Harley into her arms, unsure of what his problem was but needing to soothe him all the same. She just got him almost quiet when Josias came back into the room, a teary faced Eli next to him.

He almost wilted with relief when he saw her. "Naomi. I'm so glad you're here."

"I can see that," she quipped.

He closed his eyes briefly, shook his head. "The boys and I thought it might be a good idea to surprise you with breakfast this morning."

Naomi bit back a smile as she looked around at the disaster of the kitchen that now needed to be cleaned. "Oh, I was surprised, all right."

"We'll clean it up," Josias said.

"Tell me," she asked, her courage to carry this through leading just a bit. "Why did you want to cook me breakfast this morning?"

Josias got a sad, faraway look in his eyes. "I guess I thought if we had breakfast for you and showed you that we could handle some kitchen stuff, you would realize that it's not the only reason we want you to stay."

Her heart skipped a beat. "There are other reasons?" This was what she had stewed on all night. This was what she had been waiting for, what she had been hoping for.

"I stayed up all night," he started. Then he seemed to

think better of it and bent down to Eli. "Go sit in the living room with your brothers."

"*Jah*, Dat." Eli trudged away. And that was when Naomi saw the bandage on his arm. She could only assume that he had burned himself trying to cook her breakfast.

"Where was I?" he asked, looking back at Naomi.

"You stayed up all night," she said. But before she could say anything else, Dale came back into the house.

"The cat's back in the barn," he announced proudly.

Naomi shifted a now snoring Harley a little higher on her shoulder and gave a nod of thanks to Dale. "*Danki*," she said. "Now go back in the living room with your brothers."

"What about breakfast?"

Naomi gave him a small smile. "Don't worry about breakfast. I've got that handled. You just go and make sure your brothers don't get into any kind of bad arguments while your *dat* and I are talking."

"If you're talking," Dale started, his head tilted to one side, a shrewd look in his eyes, "how are you going to make breakfast?"

His father shot him a pointed look. "Dale. Living room. Now."

There was a split second of question, then Dale's shoulders drooped and he trudged back into the living room where his brothers waited. She could hear them knocking around in there, talking loudly and otherwise just being rowdy boys.

"Okay," Josias said. "I stayed up all night, thinking about this."

Naomi tried to adjust Harley again, but her arms were

getting tired, and one hand was falling asleep from where she had it cupped around him.

Josias must've noticed. He stopped, shook his head, then reached for the boy. She turned him over gratefully, but he stirred and whined a bit at being woken up.

"Dat," he said, swinging his legs in an attempt to be put down.

Josias set him on his feet. "Go in the living room with your brothers," he told Harley.

"*Jah*, Dat," the boy said then started in that direction.

Finally, *finally*, they were alone, and she could hear what Josias had to say. Part of her knew, deep down in her heart, she knew what he was going to say to her, but just like yesterday, she needed to hear him say it. She needed those words of affirmation from him. She needed it more than she had ever needed anything in her life.

Josias turned his blue-gray eyes to hers, his expression solemn through the smile twitching at the corners of his lips. "You don't think this is a good advertisement for what I'm about to ask you," he told her.

"Ask me anyway," she whispered.

"Naomi, yesterday I asked you to marry me, but I forgot one very important thing." He didn't have a chance to tell her what it was as a crash sounded from the living room.

Suddenly a cat came bounding through to the kitchen. Five boys came chasing after it.

"Dale, I thought I told you to put that cat outside," she called over the din. "I'll get him." Eli took off after the tiny beast.

Dale stopped chasing the cat, leaving Tommy and Harley to follow behind Eli. "I did get her out. That's a different cat."

Just how many cats were there? Many more and they would never get through this conversation.

Josias placed his thumb and his forefinger in his mouth and let out a shrill whistle, the same kind he had given her horse to get her to come to the gate of the paddock. All of a sudden the boys stopped, frozen in place even as the kitty cat scampered away out of sight.

"Do you remember what we talked about last night?" Josias asked his troop.

They all nodded vigorously.

"Then let me handle this. You stand there," he told them. "No arguing. No touching the stove. No chasing cats. No hitting your brother on the head."

That explained a lot.

"*Jah*, Dat," the boys intoned.

Once the boys seemed to be under control, Josias turned back to Naomi.

"What did you talk about last night?" she asked him, barely able to get the question out, her heart was beating so fast.

"I told them if they wanted us to be a family, then they needed to be on their best behavior."

She frowned at him. "You all are already a family."

Josias shook his head. "Most of one. But we need a *mamm*."

"That's where you come in," Dale said.

Eli approached, tugging on her dress. "Will you be our *mamm*?"

"I would love to be your *mamm*," Naomi started, "but I—"

"I love you," Josias said.

"I told you," Dale said.

"You said Naomi loved Dat," Ivan corrected. The boys started to get into an argument once more but stopped as Josias cleared his throat. "If I may continue?"

The boys straightened up, watching their father with hawk-like intensity.

"You love me?" Through all the chaos and all the time, that was what she had been longing to hear.

Josias nodded. "I realized last night I never told you that. I almost got up in the middle of the night and came to your house. But I figured your father wouldn't appreciate being woke up at two a.m."

She laughed.

He took a step toward her and clasped her hands into his own. His touch was warm and strong, and remarkably enough, Naomi could feel his love emanating toward her. It was all she ever wanted. Even if she hadn't known it until now.

"I know that art is important to you. And we'll find a way to keep it in our lives. But please, please, don't go to Philadelphia. Stay here and marry me."

Naomi gazed into those blue-gray eyes and smiled. "I would love nothing more."

From all around them, the Schrock boys cheered.

"The problem with being restless," she started, "is that you have to find someone worthy of settling down for."

* * * * *

Dear Reader,

The COVID pandemic did a number on most of us. Four-plus years later and we still are talking about what we did when we were sequestered in our own homes as we sheltered in place. As a full-time, stay-at-home author living with not one but two essential workers, my life didn't seem to change much at the time. Every now and again, the fact that we were all cooped up would make itself known to me. Those times when we wanted to celebrate out and when I couldn't get a grocery pick-up time for my order because everyone had discovered ordering groceries. Something I had been doing for years.

But that time at home changed a lot that I didn't notice, not even when we were all released. A year of staying in place and thinking about the perils of germs that we faced outside our homes shifted how most of us think about traveling and airplanes and the like.

I say all this to tell you that it's been a long time—longer than I like to think about—since I visited Kish Valley, where my new Love Inspired books are set. It is perhaps the most beautiful Amish community I have ever visited. The colorful buggies, the gorgeous mountains with the cloud-shadows traveling across the patchwork of fields. Serene, unique and simply breathtaking, Kish Valley is definitely a one-of-a-kind locale. I am so grateful that I have been able to visit there and then share stories set in this sweet little valley with you.

I may not have been back in a while, but writing these

tales takes me there, as I hope reading them does for you. So come on, let's go traveling to Kishacoquillas Valley. You don't even have to learn how to say it to enjoy it. I promise!

Always,
Amy

Get up to 4 Free Books!

We'll send you 2 free books from each series you try PLUS a free Mystery Gift.

Both the **Love Inspired®** and **Love Inspired® Suspense** series feature compelling novels filled with inspirational romance, faith, forgiveness and hope.

YES! Please send me 2 FREE novels from the Love Inspired or Love Inspired Suspense series and my FREE gift (gift is worth about $10 retail). After receiving them, if I don't wish to receive any more books, I can return the shipping statement marked "cancel." If I don't cancel, I will receive 6 brand-new Love Inspired Larger-Print books or Love Inspired Suspense Larger-Print books every month and be billed just $7.19 each in the U.S. or $7.99 each in Canada. That is a savings of 20% off the cover price. It's quite a bargain! Shipping and handling is just 50¢ per book in the U.S. and $1.25 per book in Canada.* I understand that accepting the 2 free books and gift places me under no obligation to buy anything. I can always return a shipment and cancel at any time by calling the number below. The free books and gift are mine to keep no matter what I decide.

Choose one:
- ☐ **Love Inspired Larger-Print** (122/322 BPA G36Y)
- ☐ **Love Inspired Suspense Larger-Print** (107/307 BPA G36Y)
- ☐ **Or Try Both!** (122/322 & 107/307 BPA G36Z)

Name (please print)

Address   Apt. #

City   State/Province   Zip/Postal Code

Email: Please check this box ☐ if you would like to receive newsletters and promotional emails from Harlequin Enterprises ULC and its affiliates. You can unsubscribe anytime.

Mail to the Harlequin Reader Service:
IN U.S.A.: P.O. Box 1341, Buffalo, NY 14240-8531
IN CANADA: P.O. Box 603, Fort Erie, Ontario L2A 5X3

Want to explore our other series or interested in ebooks? Visit www.ReaderService.com or call 1-800-873-8635.

---

*Terms and prices subject to change without notice. Prices do not include sales taxes, which will be charged (if applicable) based on your state or country of residence. Canadian residents will be charged applicable taxes. Offer not valid in Quebec. This offer is limited to one order per household. Books received may not be as shown. Not valid for current subscribers to the Love Inspired or Love Inspired Suspense series. All orders subject to approval. Credit or debit balances in a customer's account(s) may be offset by any other outstanding balance owed by or to the customer. Please allow 4 to 6 weeks for delivery. Offer available while quantities last.

Your Privacy—Your information is being collected by Harlequin Enterprises ULC, operating as Harlequin Reader Service. For a complete summary of the information we collect, how we use this information and to whom it is disclosed, please visit our privacy notice located at https://corporate.harlequin.com/privacy-notice. Notice to California Residents – Under California law, you have specific rights to control and access your data. For more information on these rights and how to exercise them, visit https://corporate.harlequin.com/california-privacy. For additional information for residents of other U.S. states that provide their residents with certain rights with respect to personal data, visit https://corporate.harlequin.com/other-state-residents-privacy-rights/.